naked defiance

a comedy of menace

patrik sampler

NEW STAR BOOKS

VANCOUVER
2023

NEW STAR BOOKS LTD
No. 107–3477 Commercial St., Vancouver, BC V5N 4E8 CANADA
1574 Gulf Road, No. 1517 Point Roberts, WA 98281 USA
newstarbooks.com · info@newstarbooks.com

The publisher acknowledges the financial support of the Canada Council for
the Arts, the British Columbia Arts Council, and the Government of Canada.

Cataloguing information for this book is available from Library
and Archives Canada, www.collectionscanada.gc.ca.

Cover design and typesetting by Oliver McPartlin
Printed and bound in Canada by Imprimerie Gauvin, Gatineau, QC

First printing April 2023

naked defiance

Introduction

It is a great honour to be tasked with editing this book, writing its Introduction and, moreover, to have the entire manuscript attributed to me — although I am not sure why I feel this way. Or the foundation for feeling "honoured" is somewhat unstable. Somehow it reminds me of something; perhaps an item I was reading about the fate of Jan Syrový during and after the Munich Crisis… but no, it's not quite like that. Simply, I feel a deep sense of fidelity to my publisher, and when she says, "although it sounds like we're just *asking* you to do this, really it's an order," I understand, and I comply. The fact is, no one knows who really wrote this book, but someone has to put their name on it, and it happens to be me.

When Aadesh Agarwal, owner of ████████ Books, passed away at the age of ninety-three, he bequeathed to my publisher ("bequeathed" here is more in the sense of a *reverse loan*) his entire back catalogue. This back catalogue includes a number of marginally profitable titles. (Agarwal was close personal friends with two poets laureate, and published some of their most popular work.) However, in taking on the catalogue, my publisher was contractually obliged to complete any of Agarwal's theretofore unfulfilled publishing obligations. Graciously, this happens to be just one volume, *Naked Defiance*, which you are now about to read.

The obligation to edit and publish just one book can't be too heavy for me and my publisher, who releases dozens of titles every year. Yet, as suggested above, I may at first have had some reservations about the task. For one thing, I didn't and still don't know what this book is. Is it a novel, a memoir, or something else altogether? The possibility of answering this question is confounded by my inability to ask it in the first place: there was no contact information provided for the author, the assumed name of the author (Florian Moore) appears to be a pseudonym, I can locate no such person in an international phone book, Agarwal seems to have gone to great lengths to shield the author's identity... All we have to go on is the content of a single file folder: a contract between Agarwal and the author (whose name has been redacted), the manuscript, two notes assumed to be from the author but with the signature lines torn off, another note from a copyeditor who seems to have been hired later in the editing process, likewise with the name missing, and an unattributed epilogue. The missing names made me feel some eerie feeling, and I suggested to my publisher that, under the circumstances, we might consider the contract, you know, "just a scrap of paper," as is common practice these days. My publisher, however, values her integrity, and — yes — I value my fidelity to my publisher, so...

Actually, I have overstated my difficulty in agreeing to the task. For one thing, *Naked Defiance* turns out to be quite well written. I couldn't find any typos. The sentences were all quite clear, too, which made my job easy. If this manuscript created any work for me, it was to insert the notes mentioned above in order to give the reader some insight regarding the purpose of the story — which I must say is not uninteresting. It starts with a foreword by the author, followed by the central narrative... Here I can tell you it reminds me a little bit of a children's book called *Tiddler*, about a fish who "told tall tales" — though there's always a sense the tales might be true. And in *Tiddler* we also learn the names of many kinds of fish and other sea creatures, and there's a suggestion they might also have their own take on things. Well, it's a pretty good book overall. And a nice, sweet, light story. Just like this one, and likewise well written. So, in the final equation, I suppose I don't mind having my name associated with it. And I should add that if at first I had any reservations, vanity has also won out in the end because, you know, it's simply nice to have one's name in print as an author.

Okay. Okay. If my name is associated with this book, well, I think I should say it's not merely that I "don't mind." Really, it is more than just a "pretty good" book. It's excellent. Like I wrote above, I really feel "honoured" about it. I think, perhaps, I was infected by Florian Moore's self-deprecation regarding the commercial potential of this book. You'll read what I mean in the Foreword. I don't know why he felt that way. No — this is an excellent book and I'm sure that lovers of books, in general, will come to swarm around it like insects. I think Beethoven said something like that about his Opus 38, I think it was, and this book really is that good. So I'm just really excited, as everyone says these days, to have my name on it, and I should probably go even a step farther and dedicate it to someone I admire. Emmanuel Macron is currently the president of France, and I've always wanted to have a book translated into French...

I must emphasize, however, that I'm not the real author of *Naked Defiance*. My publisher simply needed a name to attach to it, and since I was editing the book, it just made sense to use my name. She told me books sell better when readers can identify an author who takes responsibility for the words therein. Moreover, a book presenting — not entirely unfavourably — a group of people who advocate for *not buying things* (in a roundabout way, as you will read) still needs to be *sold*, if it is to get its message across. Well... let me just say that if you like the ideas in this book, I'm happy to have had some small role in bringing them to you. And if these ideas go out of fashion, just remember — again — that they're not really my ideas, and I was only doing a job.

– Patrik Sampler

Foreword

Few know the story of Naked Defiance (or just Defiance, but henceforth ND), the vaguely Marxist, anti-authoritarian art group whose existence spanned merely five years at the turn of the twenty-first century. Concerned mainly with performance art, the group invoked the influences of Dada, Surrealism, Expressionism, and — like almost every other avant-garde art movement of the previous century, whether acknowledged or not — Romanticism. Ostensibly a collective, ND was very much the project of its charismatic leader, Ganbold Mirzoyan, and disbanded within a year of his death in police custody.

At the time of Mirzoyan's death, I had a short-term contract as researcher for a registered civil society organization, and was helping to assess *post facto* the legality of his detention — of which we were made aware only through a back-page news report of an unspecified "police watchdog" investigation prompted by a man having "passed away" while in custody. This attracted the attention of our director, and I set to work gathering as much information as I could — a difficult task to say the least, given my extremely limited access to records. What little I did obtain, however, was enough for our lawyers to conclude that Mirzoyan's interactions with police had been *extrajudicial*. I believe there was little if any follow-up from our organization, although I can't be completely sure: my term concluded just days after the lawyers' assessment.

Soon I was preoccupied with a new job and new personal interests, yet a mysterious feeling lingered in me — about Mirzoyan, and his passing. My initial research had uncovered nothing more than a basic outline: he had emigrated from his birth country while in his late twenties, his sister had followed him and lived close by, he had never married, and he died in his sixth decade of life. As for employment, he had been the proprietor of a business. According to records of the local corporate registry, the business activity had been "advertising," the business name simply "MiR." It seemed to have been quite profitable, as it was later subsumed by a multinational PR firm. Judging from his home address, its sale had given Mirzoyan the funds to retire in some comfort. And yet there was hardly a trace of his passing — not even an obituary. This was strange indeed, considering he should have had a wide network of connections.

In the years that followed, I attempted to piece together a story by contacting, whenever I had some free time, anyone who may have had a connection to Mirzoyan in his later years: employees of MiR or the corporation that later acquired it, and — after some difficulty — Mirzoyan's sister. A former MiR associate informed me that Mirzoyan had for some time pursued an interest in "art performance" and I attempted to locate those who may have encountered him in this capacity. Although some had since relocated or were deceased, others were available for comment. Reticent at first, they eventually were more forthcoming and helped me understand the fuller story of ND, which is the topic of this book.

The layout of this story — the personalities involved, how one thing led to the next — is forthcoming. The broader themes, however, are what compelled me to write it. This is a story of doctrines challenged, and of great risks taken to live authentically beyond mere *surfaces* of existence. It is also the story of suppressed personal terrors, and — in some cases — lives ruined. These strike me as things we should know about, and yet they rarely enter public consciousness.

To be sure, this book will hardly count as a "public" document: you are perhaps one of only five people to hold it in their hands, never mind open the cover. Perhaps you did not seek it, but found it abandoned on the steps of an art gallery, on the seat of a bus, or on a drugstore magazine stand deceptively wrapped in the foil relief cover of a romance novel. Regardless, I ask you to keep reading.

This book — *Naked Defiance* — is the culmination of years of exhaustive research. I followed every lead, and was able to make direct contact with almost every actor who had been a part of ND. If they were deceased, I contacted their families. All interviews were conducted in person. In some cases I lived with the subjects for short periods, helping excavate parts of the story that had until then been consigned to the periphery of consciousness. In short, I sought to rebuild the story of ND with all the thoroughness I could muster, with as much painstaking personal detail as the story could withstand, in order to bring forth its true *reality*.

To take the deeply personal and make it public is the essence of *pornography*, which — at its worst — is a form of *exploitation* and proponent of the *spectacle* that members of ND strove to banish from their own lives. Here I wish to clarify my own striving to ensure that no subject was exploited (in that sense) in the undertaking of this book. I have endeavoured to protect the identities of all involved to the greatest extent possible. All names have been altered. Anagrams, perhaps? If so, I have told no one. Places have been altered. If something in reality happened at the seaside, I have set it on the shore of a lake. If it happened in a tall building, I set it underground. And I have changed all the events, too — yet the essence remains the same. Importantly, this has been achieved with the express permission of all involved. This story has gone through myriad drafts, vetted by all living subjects (and next of kin of departed subjects), and was not brought forward until all agreed that the facts presented were in fact the true facts.

Although conducting research for *Naked Defiance* was an involved process, the greatest struggle I faced was in deciding those *writerly* elements of presentation — point of view and narrative voice, in particular. For the longest time I considered a simple third-person, objective narrative. Yet somehow — instinctively — I felt such an approach would leave something out. That the story would feel more like reportage and do less to convey a better sense, for the reader, that it was a real story that really happened (because it did), and that the reader, too, might plausibly find themself, in some aspect of their life, in similar circumstances. And for this, I felt, a first-person, limited narrative was what the story needed. After all, isn't this how we really perceive the world? Yes, the story needed to be inside the mind of just one (or at least one) of the characters in order to bring forth, in veracity, the true experience of an ND actor. But who? That is, which ND actor? Whose thoughts were most appropriate to the purpose? And then, as the author — and this was perhaps the most important question — whose voice could I portray with authenticity? How could I protect *the integrity of their being*? And who would grant me permission, expressly, to use their voice?

Fortunately, as my research progressed I found myself increasingly able to identify with one actor in particular: for the purposes of this book I have named him Florian Moore. (In order to protect his family, the name "Florian Moore" is as different as I could make it from that of the real person.) Sadly, he did not survive the real-life story herein, and so I was not able to interview him in person. However, owing to the generosity of his former wife, Aïsha (again, not her real name), I was granted unlimited access to the diaries he kept during and following his involvement with ND — as well as permission to assume his voice for a story that both Aïsha and I agreed was important to tell. She was able to share with me — quite candidly — numerous anecdotes from her life with Florian Moore; the sheer amount of detail contributed in no small way to bolster my confidence in assuming his voice as first-person narrator.

In the first place, I would not have pursued Florian Moore as a potential narrative voice if it wasn't for his maleness. He was a man, I am a man. I needed this correspondence to believe in the authenticity of my portrayal. It also helped that we shared certain musical tastes. He pursued his musical interests to a far greater extent, having once been the guitarist for a vaguely *new wave* pop group that once scored a minor hit, but our record collections overlapped: Falco's *Einzelhaft*, Fripp & Eno's *Evening Star*, Simple Minds' *Empires and Dance*, etc.

What truly confirmed that I really *should* assume the voice of Florian Moore, however, was our shared genealogical ancestry. Through what at first seemed an unrelated line of questioning, I learned from Aïsha Moore that her former husband was 50 per cent Ukrainian, 37.5 per cent Irish, 9.38 per cent Czech, and 3.12 per cent Ashkenazi Jewish. That is, I discovered that Moore's genealogical ancestry had an uncanny one-to-one correspondence with my own. (To clarify, my Ukrainian ancestry comes exclusively from one parent, whereas Moore's came from both — but they add up to the same.) Learning this fact was a breakthrough in the development of this book. Certainly, I felt, these same origins, in the same proportions, must drive the same latent impulses. It was for this reason I felt I could understand, and therefore portray with some verisimilitude, the voice of Florian Moore.

I would not have proceeded, of course, without first verifying the genealogical facts. Courtesy of Moore's ex-wife I was given one of his infant teeth, which I sent to a lab for DNA testing. I did the same with a scraping from the inside of my mouth and was able to verify the corresponding ancestral proportions. Then, to further bolster my confidence, I reached out to our shared communities, and sought the endorsement of all relevant cultural institutions.

While the Federated Ukrainians demonstrated a clear lack of interest, the United Ukrainians gave an enthusiastic endorsement, inviting me to launch the book at their hall upon its completion. At the local WISE hall, Irish representatives arranged for an elaborate induction ceremony in which I was wrapped in a damp sod carpet while onlookers drank ceremonial ale and performed chants in Gaeilge. At the Honorary Consulate of the Czech Republic I was given a box of souvenir spa wafers. The rabbi at a local synagogue told me 3.12 per cent was a "negligible amount" and that I could "do what [I] want." While this was not, perhaps, an *unqualified* endorsement, it nevertheless gave me full confidence to proceed. And this was, alas, well-placed confidence.

As the writing process got underway, my belief in the deeper meaning of our shared origins was confirmed. I found myself largely empathizing with Moore's responses to the stimuli in his surrounding environment; with his role, characterized more often than not by a *lack of agency*, in ND. As the story unfolds, this meaning should become clear. Suffice it to say, *lack of agency* characterizes the way I felt during my term with the "registered civil society organization" mentioned above. Perhaps all of us have felt, at some point in our lives, as if we were just being carried along by some unstoppable machine, and that some part of its mechanism had been shielded from us. Regardless: I should emphasize that I would not have reached the same ideological conclusions as Florian Moore — nor do I condone them. (This is a topic I will set aside for the time being.)

What follows is the story of Naked Defiance, a pseudo-Marxist art group at the turn of the twenty-first century, as seen through the eyes of one of its members, latecomer Florian Moore. Their story is the story of our age — an age of internecine distractions in a crumbling environment, if I can be so blunt. I dedicate this book to their struggles against this current, and to their admittedly limited accomplishments. Far more often than not, such endeavours have been occluded by the spectacular fraud of what we might call "consumer capitalism" — or of its attending curtailments of the human spirit, in any event. I dedicate this book to all whose significance — whose right to exist, buffeted by the violence of the spectacle — has been consigned to the backwaters of memory. And I write it at the very end of the world — or what looks like the very end of the world. That is to say I write it defiantly, hopefully.

(From this point forward, disregard the *author* in this first-person narrative; hereon I assume the voice and perceptions of *Florian Moore*.)

SPRING

1

It was still early in the year; the forest fires weren't yet burning. The air was airy, dominated neither by the hotness of heat nor the coldness of cold. It had both those things. It was like stirring ice through a pot of boiled water by hand. Humid. And the light was luminescent, filtered directly before my eyes by the new, thin green leaves of alder. Beyond that was the steel-grey sea, occasional glints of reflected light. This was what the leaves filtered, I thought. The sun was somewhere behind me to the left. The sky was very light blue, and there were traces of lifting mist.

Descending a staircase. Or just stairs. Wood planks, or wood frames packed with soil. Someone told me years ago there were nine hundred and ninety-nine of them. I had lost count. I hadn't been counting. A metal sign bolted to a wood post: "Clothing optional at beach ahead." There were now perhaps just a dozen… a dozen dozen stairs left. I felt for the instruction card in my shirt pocket. Someone — I don't know who — had left it for me in a specified location, where I picked it up just days before. I had it memorized, but wanted to make sure. Like the engineer of a Japanese train who points with a white-gloved hand at each gauge on the dashboard — to make sure. And soon enough I was there on the smooth stones of the backshore. I was to remove all my clothes. I had agreed to it. To whatever was there on the instruction card. This was my induction. Or was it a hazing ritual? At the back of my mind I considered whether it was an elaborate joke, a humiliation. But no — this is what they do. This is how I show my commitment, how I meet them for the first time. Furthermore, I thought, it shouldn't feel so strange to remove my clothes at a nude beach.

Now I walked straight ahead to the foreshore. There were little waves that, at just the right angle of refraction, gave fleeting windows to the nearshore bottom: flat sand, fewer of the smooth stones. In my peripheral vision I was looking for someone making the same moves at the same time, perhaps one hundred meters down the shore to my left. They shouldn't be hard to find as I had spotted perhaps only five other beach goers, all seated. It was 10:37 a.m., the time indicated on the card. And there they were in my peripheral vision, walking like me, matching my speed, right to the foreshore. Next I turned counter clockwise and they — *she* — turned clockwise, I could see her now but pretended not to be looking. Next we returned slowly to the backshore. The instructions were to remove our clothes in a certain order and to place them on the nearest convenient dry surface — if at all possible, a log.

Seated, facing the ocean, I removed my shoes and socks, neatly placed my socks inside my shoes, stood up, turned around, and placed them on the log I had found. Following our directions, next we removed whatever garments covered our legs, held them up before us, folded them neatly, set them down. Then our lower body undergarments. The same. My skin that almost never touched the outdoor air was now washed with a sudden breeze that pressed the tail of my shirt to my buttocks and brushed the hairs of my scrotum, which had tightened in response to the ambient temperature. Now I was unbuttoning my shirt. The shirt came off my shoulders. I folded it, and set it down. Now I was completely exposed but for the brimmed hat. I felt the air and the weak sun on my chest, and I wondered what she was feeling those one hundred meters — less, perhaps — down the shore. In response to the air, to the light, the instructions…

We turned again toward the shore, and in doing so faced one another briefly. I was to be — we were to be, although I hadn't seen her instruction card, the objects and not the subjects of this performance; the ones seen, but not the ones looking. If seen by anyone, my job was to appear not to be looking, and yet I did look, while doing my best to appear as if my gaze were unfocussed. Whether I had the skill to give this impression, I am not sure. Regardless, I was curious to see this naked stranger, and I gazed directly at her, if only for a fleeting off-script moment.

At such a distance, my interlocutor was too far to identify, and she was likely a stranger anyway. I saw only those details that are easy to recognize from such a distance: hair length and approximate colour, body proportions, facial profile. Not close enough to see those other features that would tell me, for example, her age: the depth of wrinkles around the eyes, skin texture, strands of grey hair (or not). I could see she tended toward the athletic, and her proportions were such that even a few decades would not make much difference. She could be anywhere between twenty and fifty, I thought. And what would she think of me from that distance, if she were to care? What would anyone see, if they were looking? I have been told I look young for my age…

According to the instructions, we were now walking very slowly — "mindfully" was the word — back to the water. That is, each footstep was intentional and meditative. I was to consider the intensity of pressure at each location on the sole of each foot pressing into the stones, the sand; to consider the geological history of the stones, the sand. There had been billions of years leading to this moment. The instructions assumed the reader was a spiritualist, suggested posterity, an oceanic connection to those billions of years. Billions of years during which geology was nothing to me, or I was nothing to geology — until now.

But there was also a suggestion of menace, an emphasis on this moment, the unexpected deviation of one person in geological time, now the swiftly occluding transience of human beings and other living things — although I noticed hopefully, again, that the forest fires weren't yet burning.

We were walking to the water, almost there. Following directions, I leaned down and placed my hat on the foreshore, stood up, and faced my interlocutor. She removed her hat and waved to me with it, exaggeratedly joyful, then threw it up the shore. I waved back. Her expression — was it in the script? It was unselfconscious yet seemed perfectly choreographed. She had as they say *stage presence*, and I had noticed in my peripheral vision that each move of hers down to the shore lacked any hesitation. She must be, I thought, a dancer or a circus performer when she's not doing this. That should not have been at all surprising — to find an artist making art. I had once been a musician...

The water was cold as we slowly submerged ourselves in unison. Having exposed that section of my body so rarely, I imagined the gaze of the audience (did anyone notice us?) there. Once submerged to my navel I was more able to focus on my object nature and physical sensations on the body; on the instrument for this performance. Sand on soles, water running between the digits of my feet, the cooling of my knees, water pushing at my thighs in alternating direction, water surrounding buoyant genitals, water rising and falling smoothly on torso leaving a damp expanse extra-cooled by the breeze, hands in the water, water running through fingers, breeze on my chest, on my face...

Submerged to the shoulders, I observed at eye level each crest and trough of what appeared to be a respiratory stationary wave. Whether it was in fact stationary, I lacked the knowledge to confirm. It did seem very much like breathing, however. I often see the ocean this way; as a unitary breathing organism. A nurturing and circulating organism, yet also eerily indifferent. Perceiving it this way reminds me of Stanisław Lem's sentient yet somehow aloof planet *Solaris* — although I haven't read the book in years.

The instructions on the card contain a number of thoughts for the performer, although not much in the way of physical movement from this point forward — other than to return to shore, to dress, to leave. This, my first action with Defiance, was so subtle that anyone who observed it might not have recognized it as a performance, as art. That, I understood, was the point: to bring the unexpected to the unsuspecting, never to announce an action as such, only to make quotidian life mildly stranger.

We, the performers, arrived separately and had to leave separately. I went the same way I came, but not so expeditiously. Near the base of the stairs there were flowers—some kind of aster. There were ferns. And rhododendron-like shrubs. In the leaves of one of these I noticed pea-like growths. I understood these to be galls—not fruit or seeds, but outgrowths incubating larvae. Later, on the bus home, I noticed a number of women who might have fit the description of my partner at the beach.

2

Some months prior to my first action with Defiance, I had been invited by an old friend to see a movie. Gavin, who I first met in a studio art course at university, had since gone on to work in the film industry — variously as a cinematographer on some small-budget documentaries, and as a line producer for a number of mid-budget showbiz-oriented movies. He knew I had little patience for the latter, and admitted that the movie he wanted me to see was in his words "exactly not your kind of film." But it contained, he said, one "noteworthy event" that had to be seen in context.

Dynamite II (titled *Blown Up* in some release markets) features Páll Dengler — in his second starring role for German action film director Heinz Schreiber — as a New York police detective investigating a series of explosions at the homes of wealthy socialites. Concurrently, a well-connected photographer has noticed that the victims of these explosions all happen to be people he has recently photographed at weddings and other public events. Troubled by this connection, the photographer is thrust into a deep ontological crisis, and asks himself, "Am I causing this? Am I the Devil?" He is somewhat relieved to be brought in for questioning after Dengler draws a similar conclusion. However, despite the photographer readily proclaiming his guilt and expressing relief that "the Devil" has finally been apprehended, Dengler remarks to the police commissioner — a cameo played by well-known Shakespearian actor Alasdair Wickets — that "Something just doesn't feel right about this."

Here the dramatic irony intensifies as the audience is made aware the villain is in fact a photo lab technician who has been choosing victims from the images he prints for the society photographer. As his plans become more devious — among other things, he has hidden a small missile launcher within a 500mm telephoto lens — the race is now on to catch the villain before he can get to his next planned victim: the daughter of New York's mayor. Here, in a flashback, we are prompted to have some empathy for the photo lab technician: we learn that he was raised in poverty by his widowed mother, that his father was killed in an industrial accident resulting from a rich and powerful factory owner's callous disregard for safety — thus his hatred for the rich. (In publicity for the film, Schreiber said he wanted it to be "a meditation on inequality in American society.")

When Dengler finally pieces things together, the photo lab technician is already on the highway in his battered pickup truck, heading in the direction of the mayor's daughter's suburban mansion. Realizing this, Dengler gets into his Chevrolet Camaro Z28 and races to intercept the truck, weaving in and out of traffic. Once he catches up, the photo lab technician starts lobbing grenades and sticks of dynamite out of the truck's back window, where they slide across the open tailgate and land on the road. Dengler, in his Camaro, has to slalom between explosions. Finally, crossing a construction site, the truck hits a large bump, and the tailgate bounces shut just as the technician lobs his last grenade. The grenade gets trapped in the back of the truck, which explodes in midair as it sails off an unfinished highway overpass. Dengler returns to the jail where the photographer is being held, opens his jail cell door, and says to him, "Now I know you're not the Devil."

Schreiber ("a nice guy, but a moron," according to Gavin) went quite quickly through the nine-million-dollar budget allotted for the film (of which it earned back only forty thousand) and the producers, frustrated by numerous broken deadlines, told him he wouldn't get a cent more — which is what led to the "noteworthy event" Gavin wanted me to see. As it turns out, Schreiber was an obsessive fan of Alasdair Wickets, although the feeling wasn't mutual; Schreiber had had to beg him to play the role of the police commissioner. And since these scenes were filmed toward the end of production, Schreiber had already run out of the somewhat expensive fee he was contractually obliged to pay him.

At the time Wickets was eighty years old, at the end of his career, and in no need of money. He had also, according to Gavin, become quite taken with a certain group of underground "art radicals," and was quite interested to pursue their agenda. Seeing an opportunity, he offered to have his fee waived on the following condition: that in one of his scenes he would be allowed to look directly into the camera and say "Blap!" before continuing as scripted. When Schreiber asked him why, Wickets told him it was something had always dreamed to do, just once in his career — that he would be extremely pleased if allowed to make this move in the great director's film. Flattered and thankful, nevertheless confused, Schreiber agreed.

I told Gavin I never failed to be disappointed and mystified by the intense gap between money spent on unworthy versus worthy art (that is, the higher amounts going to the former), that I was at the same time "deeply impressed" by Wickets' gesture in *Dynamite II*, and that I would like to know more about the "art radicals" he mentioned.

"I can put you in contact, if you'd like," he said.

3

Some were nude. Some were clothed. Among the nude, more were men. Fewer nude than clothed, overall. A small number were simply topless — perhaps testing how they might feel to go fully nude. A couple — a man and a woman in their early 30s, I guessed — began the party merely topless, then completely disrobed. I overheard her tell him it "wasn't fair" there was nothing at all provocative about a man not wearing a shirt. The party's host had announced it would be clothing-optional, although he hadn't taken the option. Like him, I kept my clothes on: it was my first time at a Defiance gathering, after having gained access via my performance at the beach. Nudity, I thought, made more sense outdoors, especially if it were secondary to some kind of physical activity: swimming, playing volleyball. Standing and talking was a different category.

I knew no one at the party. I expected to know no one. Any fear of awkwardness, however, soon dissipated. There was a garden; an immediate topic of conversation. The host, Ganbold Mirzoyan — I noticed almost everyone introduced themselves by their full names — greeted me and brought me, along with other recently arrived guests, on a brief tour of the house. It was a shoes-off house, so we carried our shoes right through to the back porch — from which we could see the tops of surrounding distant mountains.

Ganbold asked how I had found out about Defiance. I told him how I happened to see *Dynamite II*. "Oh yes, the 'BLAP!'" he said, adding that he had been "thrilled" to have Alasdair Wickets involved. I asked if Wickets was still taking part, and was told the stunt had been just a "one-off." Wickets was a busy man, Ganbold said. "Even at his advanced age he has a lot — maybe too much, even — to keep himself occupied. I don't know how he does it."

In the downward-sloping back yard, Ganbold showed us his garden. There were raised planting beds constructed of interlocking timber. One of these was filled entirely with Lacinato kale — it grows well anywhere, he told us — and the others with a mixture. There were some new lettuces, carrots just coming up. There were five apple saplings, newly planted. He grew them from seed, he told us, from apples of an indeterminate variety taken from an abandoned orchard some years ago. "I have no idea what I'm doing, whether this is a good spot to grow them," he admitted. In one corner of the yard was a flowering currant bush with Anna's hummingbirds occasionally darting in and out. The ground was mostly mulch, and the entire space was made private by pink-flowering salmonberry bushes on all sides. Thanks to the bushes and surrounding trees — alder, a few cedar — one could garden in the nude without causing offence, he pointed out. There were other houses nearby, but none could be seen from the back yard thanks to the foliage, and the size of the lots. We asked about the tall wire fencing, not far beyond the salmonberry walls. Deer fences, they were still well within the property lines, not to take too much away from the animals, he told us.

As for the house itself, it was in what one might call "good taste," especially compared to some other houses in the neighbourhood, which seemed to have been designed for people with *no taste* only in the interest of consuming money. Indisputably, Ganbold's house also gave the impression of wealth — I overheard someone hush, "Where did he get his money?" and confirmed later that the source was an advertising or PR business. But ostentation was clearly not the point of his home's design. It was not grotesquely large — not large at all — and it was, overall, *comfortable.* The main floor was a continuous plane of uniform wood flooring extending from the entrance — which he called the *genkan* — through the living area and kitchen to the balcony. There were heavy walls, but also light partitions of frosted glass or paper. One felt neither exposed nor isolated on this floor. I thought it the kind of space Frank Lloyd Wright might have designed after a research trip to Japan. There was a lot of wood, and the open kitchen had some countertops made from single slabs of varnished timber. I remember light reflecting off the balcony, refracting through the tumblers set for guests.

At some point we all — slightly less than twenty of us, I think — assembled in the main living area. There were two sofas, chairs were brought in, but some chose to sit on the floor. The unclothed sat on their folded clothes, or towels brought for the purpose. As I would learn was the custom, each meeting began with a restatement of our mission. This time Ganbold took the responsibility — it seemed there was consensus to defer to the host — and reminded us that when our group was formed there were at first specific tactics, but that an overarching strategy took time to identify. Someone called the essence of this strategy "defiance," and so that became our name.

We oppose meaningless convention, said Ganbold, thus some of us are unclothed. If there is a utility or pleasure in wearing clothes we wear them. But we embrace freedom, so no one says, "You must wear clothes." We oppose, too, miserabilism—the miserabilism of ecophobia and the cyborg body. We move in physical space and we are able to look one another in the eyes, unmediated. We reject the cult of the car and move with our own bodies. We see ourselves as just one kind of animal, with no more rights than any other kind of animal. We oppose the passive nihilism of "business as usual" that is destroying life on this planet, and we embrace active nihilism, rejecting all that has no true value. We embrace the surprise, and reserve the right to surprise others. In short, we love life — real life, not refracted life. There is nothing, nothing we abhor more than the unreal spectacle.

If I may have your indulgence, indulge myself, deviate from our regular incantation... Simply, I wish to admit my guilt. Namely, that I profited off the spectacle for so many years — at least two decades by my estimate. If I could excuse myself, I would say it was merely a matter of survival. As a result, now I want for nothing. Perhaps now I live within what the planet allows me — I believe this is true, although I am not entirely certain. What I admit is that I used the spectacle. I had advantages. It was a ladder — but a soul-crushing ladder.

As you know, our countries were declared enemies. I wasn't free there. I was a poet and I wasn't free. The authorities saw to it that I would never be published. My narrative didn't match theirs. Well, let me just say I don't know how great they were, my poems. Not bad, certainly, but not Coleridge, either. But here, you see, the spectacle of the dissident of an enemy state was my ticket to freedom — or at least to material sustenance. Did anyone here really care about my poetry? Not really. I sold some books here, but few of my readers knew the difference between good poetry and bad poetry — or between poetry and a tax invoice, for that matter. If they bought my book, they were interested only in the dissident as commodity. They were glad for the proof that someone from over there had chosen to live here; that things here really were better than they were over there. And as someone who had been frustrated in my own country — and who embraced the idea that my enemy's enemy is my friend — I was more than happy to play the role. And for the relative stability and material comfort, I should add. My point being that I had an advantage — an unfair advantage, I think. I was simply born in the right place at the right time. I don't think someone like me would have the same advantages now. Material advantages, especially. And that's fair enough, I suppose. I ramble. What I want to say is that I used the spectacle as a ladder, but it was more deeply insidious. The spectacle became everything.

I think you know that after coming here I built a life on selling images — of selling lies. I knew about words, about signs, about images… and in this country, if you know about those things you are compelled to use them for PR. Or if you know about those things you might simply not use them and make your living otherwise. But if you want to use them for your livelihood, that's what you do. And then your entire life revolves around selling things and your entire life becomes a lie. My life became a lie. I was just some happy face balloon who sold plastic junk to children through their parents. Or to parents through their children — I don't know which. Sold planet-heating vacations to not-fully-formed adults chasing the 'S's of tourism at interchangeable overseas resorts. All the while justifying this work, somehow. It must have taken some mental effort. What I can confirm is that I had become an image-trading systems manager. I was completely empty, and eventually — why it took so long, I am unsure — I came to know it. I concluded I had been duped into exchanging one kind of unfreedom for another. My balloon was ever-expanding with inauthenticity. And then it popped. I revolted completely.

That is to say, I want you to know my shame. Know, too, that this feeling of shame intensifies my belief in what we are doing here, and my gratitude to all who are involved. I know we all came here on different paths, and that many of you had always been aware — I thank you for your acceptance. Regardless of how we arrived, we are united in opposing the spectacle. We will not be the spectacle. We are insurgents of the marvellous. If we can't convince the miserable to seek surprises — to seek life — we bring surprises to them. As the world chokes on its own mental sewage, we will be a Heimlich maneuver for the mind...

After Ganbold restated our purpose, we arranged ourselves in small, randomized groups. Someone provided a deck of cards — each card depicted an animal, I think they were from a children's game — and we located partners holding the same card. With our partners, we discussed possible "actions." These were to be conducted in public settings, yet never announced as "performances," so as to subvert the spectacle. And we needed to be mindful of the safety of the actors: none of our actions could expose the actors to physical injury, nor could they be illegal. Working in small groups provided oversight, and once our actions had been composed, they were typed out using old-fashioned typewriters — to preclude the recognition of anyone's handwriting — and sealed in envelopes. Turns were taken at the typewriters — three were brought for this particular meeting — and the din of typing, from various corners, lasted perhaps an hour. The actions were sealed in envelopes, on which performance dates were likewise typed. Toward the end of the evening these envelopes were distributed face down, and further exchanged if one was not available on the indicated date. The process was congenial. Whatever "action" I helped create that night is immaterial. Simply, I had input; I was impressed by the insights of my interlocutors; and I felt quite strongly, *I am among good people*. It was rare to feel this way, and I began to understand Ganbold's feeling of indebtedness.

4

The meeting ended and the party continued. I was inspecting the tree rings of a countertop formed from a single slab of varnished timber, there to take a tumbler, to get a drink. People here weren't big drinkers, I concluded. There was just one bottle of wine — a Pinot Gris, if I remember correctly — hardly touched. There were quite a few bottles of sparkling water. What did I need? There were potluck items, too. While considering what to drink, I might take a plate, I thought. My contribution: some crackers and a vegan paté — neither original nor time consuming. There was an assortment of home-made items. One was a loaf of bread. I had noticed its arrival in a *furoshiki* — quaint, I thought — transported by a young woman (late 20s?) who arrived not long after me. She was wearing a quilted bomber-style jacket, which Ganbold gallantly took from her shoulders, and a knee-length cotton dress, which dropped to the floor as soon as she alighted from the *genkan*. She had been wearing nothing underneath. And now she was with him again, standing with a drink in hand, talking, earnest. Somewhere at the other side of the main room.

"Quite fetching, don't you think?"

The voice was close and took me by surprise — not merely because it was close, but also because the tone was so bold. Ganbold and the young woman were across the room to my right. The voice was to my left. A woman's voice. Was she referring to them? Had she noticed my wandering attention? I turned to the left. She — the voice — had a round face with a sharp, smooth, almost beak-like nose. A small chin. I would say she was uniquely pretty — just a few millimetres on the side of pretty. Her brown eyes — crow's feet indicating a certain age, perhaps late 30s — motioned over to Ganbold and his partner. I considered my answer, thought it best to be circumspect.

"I'd say they're both quite handsome," I replied.

"She's certainly taken a liking to him."

"Well, it seems they get along quite well."

"Women find it easy to talk with him. He's quite straightforward. You know, in that disarming way only men with accents can pull off. When a language isn't your own, you can operate it at a distance. Say what you think and feel no shame. He can say something obscene or vulgar, but he probably doesn't feel it — nor does it sound that way to us, spoken in that accent."

"Well, he does have a kind of manly charm."

"Yes. A certain stature, tone of voice. But you have much nicer eyes," she said.

"Are you flirting with me?"

"No. I'm not."

"If there's a man here whose eyes —"

"Ganbold?"

"Yes."

"He has an intense gaze. He's very forceful. I don't always follow his logic, although I agree with the premise. But he can make you believe that what we're doing is the right thing. That between the way he sees things and what others don't see, there's a space and... well, that's not the same. With your eyes it's more..." At this she looked quite directly at my eyes. "It's more... They're far away, your eyes. I imagine a lot of women want to make them look even more distant, less focussed... In a caring, respectful way, of course."

"You are flirting with me."

"I'm simply stating an objective fact. I have no reason to flirt because I'm happily married. I'm a housewife — right now. I am very busy, I can assure you, and I don't have time to flirt, or try out any new sex moves."

"It's just as well. I'm married, too. And I think I'd find it simply too emotionally conflicting to cheat. I've never tried it, and I don't think I care to."

"That's good. Oh — I should also tell you... I'm newly pregnant."

"Congratulations."

"I'm not sure if we can really congratulate someone on being pregnant — at this point in history."

"I tend to agree. I've been a parent for seven years now. I certainly don't regret it, but —"

"By the way, my name is Haruko." She reached out her hand.

"Haruko." We shook hands.

"Haruko Rusakova. It's my married name."

"I'm Florian. Moore is the last name."

"You know we've met before, don't you?"

"We have?"

"I think so. At the beach, I believe. And —"

"It was you! Yes, I did think you looked familiar, somehow. It was my first action."

"I thought so. I hadn't noticed you here before."

"I'm sure I looked quite amateur. Compared to you. You must be in theatre or dance — professionally, I thought."

"I am. Some theatre friends put me on to Defiance. How did you find out?"

"Well, I had been a musician, but haven't been involved in anything creative in quite a while — especially since having children. An old music friend introduced me to Ganbold."

"You were looking for an outlet."

"Yes. I think not having one... It wasn't really good for me. And ruminating about the state of the world. I hadn't made anything, really, in years."

To clarify my work as a musician, I mean I had once been in a *pop music group*. Musicianship was part of it, undoubtedly. We were all quite accomplished musicians. Our bass player and drummer were self-taught, but quite technically skilled — any resentment I held toward our bassist was tempered by my awe at his speed and subtlety. The keyboardist was studying for a university music degree, which he finished about a year before our band broke up. I had been playing guitar and taking music lessons from about the age of fifteen. I was also the singer and main lyricist.

Our style was hard to place — we wanted it to be hard to place. We were working at a time when music fans were looking for novelty, musical miscegenation — or at least that's what the music industry was promoting at the time. Working then was an advantage for us, considering our musical interests. We were merging a variety of influences — progressive rock, Italo disco, some of that motorik German stuff. We had some Chic albums, some Eno albums. Genesis' *Foxtrot* was something we listened to a lot as well, although I'm not sure why. We played a lot in time signatures other than 4/4, but we were into minimalism.

Clearly it was all about the music for us. I wanted it to be more about the music. But I also understood that to make our work self-sustaining — I mean financially self-sustaining — we needed to play the game, to be part of the spectacle that is at least fifty percent of everything in the music business. I was probably the most determined — I took care of most of the promotion — but we all worked hard. We were always playing gigs, sometimes driving quite far to do so, and spending most of our disposable cash recording — and it was expensive to record in those days. Our demo tapes were getting out and we were making contacts. It always felt we were getting closer. Our name was getting around. I overheard complete strangers talking about us at a pub one night. Record labels told us they liked our sound — that we had great "sonic textures" and such — but to send them our next thing. The truth was this: we sounded great, but none of our songs were particularly *catchy*.

Then one day Gerrit, our keyboardist, dropped a beer on the keys of his Korg MS-20. It was the start of a jam session and we were just testing our sound levels. Rubin, the bassist, was playing a mock funk riff and the keyboardist was about to open a can of beer just retrieved from our ice chest. Fortunately not yet open, it slipped out of his hands and bounced across the keys. When we were reviewing the tape it was the best thing there — the accidental bass and synth interplay. Because Gerrit had so much musical training, he had never been very spontaneous. But finally — thanks to a slippery can of beer — he came up with the riff we needed. We were laughing — not at the accident, but because what we heard was so uncannily, surprisingly infecting. It put us in high spirits. Our musical training came into play as we worked on the arrangement, and I came up with some lyrics — light-hearted, almost a parody of some of the R&B stuff we heard floating around in those days. The song would be called "Turn On the Lights (I Like to Watch)." It was sly — right on the line between ultra-commercial and ultra-weird. We felt it had enough of the latter that we could maintain our integrity.

After recording a demo version, we sent it off to an A&R guy with whom we had built some rapport. He could see potential in the song, but I think he admired our persistence even more, and wanted to give us a break. From what I understand, it took some convincing on his part to get the record label to agree, but finally we had a recording contract. It was for three singles, and there were some conditions: we had to take direction from the label's in-house producer — a guy who had normally worked with run-of-the-mill pop-rock acts — and we had to change our name. The label's director felt that Hidden Lights was too bland. We brainstormed some options, even cut out letters and rearranged them on a tabletop. We thought it seemed too throw-away, but the director took a liking to Rondo X.

On the financial side, the contract didn't favour us: all production debts had to be paid off before we saw any profit, and our cut after that was only nine percent. But this was the only offer we had, and after a solid five years of hard work we felt we had to take it. Perhaps I pushed harder than the rest of the band, but I think we all felt we weren't going to get anything better. The label convinced us by pointing out that we didn't have the capacity to do all the distribution and publicity on our own — especially to an overseas market, where they felt our sound would be better received.

In the studio the song retained its essence. The producer understood us better than we thought he would, but insisted on some obvious commercial touches, suggesting some more familiar-sounding fills for our drummer, Marc, who was used to showing off a bit more. For my guitar I was asked, in the producer's words, to "turn down the Fripp and turn up the Rodgers" — as in Robert Fripp and Nile Rodgers. And instead of my bandmates singing the backing vocals, they brought in a girl for this purpose — almost a girl: she was just eighteen or nineteen years old, I think. The daughter of the label's local distribution manager, who had been looking to give her a break. She sang the line, "I like to watch." She made it sound flirty, so we embellished a bit, adding an extra line, "You know I like to watch you, baby." Her name was Aggy, and she was very good — precociously wise, like a musician with many more years' experience. She could do a lot with her voice, and she had charisma, too.

Aggy made the song, really. Her addition gave it that final push that suggested a hit. And she made the video, too. We had been promised a video, and we got one — just not the way we thought. The label got us an appearance on a local breakfast TV show, where we lip-synched our song in front of a blue screen. It was done "live" in one take without any of us obviously messing up — and we looked great. We all got new haircuts for the occasion. Marc, Rubin, and I each had some variation of what I would later come to know as "anime hair" — big, spiky. Mine was red. Gerrit had an asymmetrical jet-black bob, shaved on one side. Lots of eye makeup. Aggy was more-or-less natural looking save for heavy eyeliner. We had lots of leather. She had a red lamé dress — and insisted on bare feet so she could "move properly." There was one stationary and two roving cameras. One roved all over Aggy in particular. It was clear she really caught the cameraman's interest on her side of the stage. The label got copies of the tapes, told us they liked what they saw, did some minor editing, gave us a video. A video on the cheap. We were expecting something more, but as our A&R guy said, "It wasn't like we were going to fly you all to Sri Lanka." We should have been relieved — we were paying for it, after all.

Any disappointment was briefly assuaged when "Turn On the Lights" had some chart success in its first test market, Switzerland, peaking at 81. Not long after that it was released in Benelux, where it got to 53 in Belgium and 20 in the Netherlands. It was a strange few months in my life. There was the excitement of having a hit single — yes, we could legitimately say it was a hit, if it were number 20 in the Netherlands — but having virtually no recognition at home. Our gigs were more sparsely attended than ever. The name change was probably confusing for those who had known us as Hidden Lights, and I'm sure there were those who simply thought we had sold out — which we had. I imagine those who came to see Rondo X were surprised that Aggy wasn't in fact a part of the band. (Rubin and Gerrit sang her lines when we played "Turn on the Lights" live.) The singer from a big-name band on our label had given us a plug in an NME interview — but the label turned us down for an opening spot when they came to town. When we asked about touring Benelux, the label told us they'd take a "wait and see" approach. Any hope of that, however, ended when the follow-up single, "Get Shy," failed to chart at all.

"Get Shy" had been written on some poor advice: that we should simply reproduce the formula for the first single. So we played the same riff but backward — literally in reverse. There was no video, and I can't confirm there was any promo, either. To be fair to the label, they had taken us on board only at the tail-end of our musical era. Quite rapidly, audiences were walking toward purism, segregating themselves into either rock or techno. Our style of music was rapidly becoming a thing of the past. Within a few short years, guitars and synthesizers would no longer be seen together on the same stage — and it was to stay that way for at least a decade. I understand that side of things now, but at the time all I saw was our label's neglect, which was also certainly real. In any event, we knew we weren't going to get a second contract, so decided to do just what we wanted for the third single, the very strange and tossed-off sounding "Ms. La La at the Circus," named for the Degas painting. Again, it had virtually no promo. It surprised both us and our label when it broke the top 100 (got to 93, to be precise) in Belgium, its only release market. But that was the end of our career. We were all very burned out at this point, disillusioned, and not getting along too well, either. We played a final gig to little fanfare and disbanded.

When Hidden Lights — or Rondo X — broke up, I was twenty-six. I had devoted roughly a fifth of my life to the band.

It had been real, obsessive devotion. Virtually every waking thought — and my dreams, too — had been about honing my craft, and attempting to make it big. It was as if I had been rubbing some twigs together interminably long, finally getting a spark, some smoke, and then — poof — nothing. Some strike it lucky right away, but many don't. By the time we see someone accomplish something — no matter how minor — they may have spent years building up to it. For maybe a week of excitement. When "Turn on the Lights" hit the charts, it really was just a week of feeling — excuse the cliché — like I was walking on air. But that was it. What came after was pure frustration, really. Then the band broke up, and all I had was my day job at a health food warehouse. To be sure, I also had an undergrad degree in art history (worth less than the warehouse job) and was able to teach guitar lessons on the side. But that was about it.

A few years after Rondo X, Gerrit put out a joke concept album called *Feelings of the Ass*, told ostensibly from the perspective of a donkey. Released on vinyl, its cover image was a painting — a poorly rendered mule and a disproportionately large human hand on a fantasy landscape. I took it as a snub dismissing some of my loftier ideas. Marc continued drumming for various bands around town, and eventually moved overseas with a foreign girlfriend. Rubin had been dating an exotic dancer known as Open Flower, and not long after Rondo X they formed a rap-metal band called Sucky Charger. Rubin grew dreadlocks, got all tatted up, and from then on played a lot of slap bass. Open Flower, on vocals, sang screamy lyrics with lots of double entendre, employed her erstwhile stage experience during live shows. Drums and guitar — fairly standard thrash metal — filled out the sound. It was the antithesis of Rondo X. Sucky Charger never had any radio hits, but they had steady album sales and were able to make a living playing festivals and doing their own tours. I hated their music, but have to admit I was a bit envious at their success. If I'm being honest, I can say Rubin was the only one of us who had any business sense — which isn't the same as integrity.

After Rondo X, I had had enough, and quit making my own music. Aside from teaching guitar in the evening, I maintained no connection to music. At the warehouse I moved into a management position with higher wages and more demands on my time. I held on to all my gear — effects pedals, rhythm machines, amps — expecting my interest to relapse. After a few years, however, I conceded it was all just collecting dust, and started to sell it off. One of the biggest purchases of my Hidden Lights years had been a Roland TR-808 rhythm machine. Aside from my Fender Stratocaster, it was my favourite piece of musical equipment — hard to part with. At that time, however, the TR-808 was getting quite trendy among techno freaks, and I thought I could get a good price for it — higher than I paid, possibly. And this is how I met Aïsha. She answered my ad for the 808 on a local buy and sell website and came over to test it out. If two people seduce each other through music lessons, the movie cliché would involve the piano or the guitar. But why not a rhythm machine? Let me say I have never been so infected by another's love for an instrument's sound. The TR-808 became hers, but she came back many times for programming advice, to talk about music, listen to records. And now we have two young children.

Aïsha was a better sound engineer than I had ever been, although she wasn't as seduced by the spectacle of pop music. Out of practicality she completed a nursing degree, and between our two jobs we lived comfortably. Music, for Aïsha, was always purely for the love of music. She had production credits for some local bands, but was never motivated to promote her own work. I, on the other hand, did find myself drawn back to the spectacle, and this led to some regret and humiliation.

Inevitably the age of rock purism faded and there was a revival of music from the same era as Hidden Lights and Rondo X. Other bands of the time had released remixes of past hits with some success, and I thought I could do the same. Because the label owned the recording and wasn't interested, I decided to re-record "Turn on the Lights" on my own. I thought the internet would take care of the promo — but I had clearly misjudged public memory of our one hit. All I had accomplished was to annoy my former bandmates (I hadn't told them of my plans), waste money, and use up more space in Aïsha and my now cramped apartment: to this day, I still have a stack of unsold CDs and 12" singles.

I gave Haruko the outline of my story in music — no names, just the most important events — and concluded, "I still get an airplay royalty cheque now and again. Perhaps every year or two years, for about the same amount as a meal in a fast-food restaurant."

To this, she replied: "Yeah, so do I."

"You were a musician, too?"

"The band you were in was called Rondo X, if I'm not mistaken."

"How do you know — ?"

"Florian, take a good look. Are you really sure you don't recognize me?"

Author's First Note to Publisher

The following passage was supplied with a brief note by the author addressed to "Mr. Agarwal." In this missive, the author suggests the passage "might be inserted as-is between chapters 4 and 5" and offers to make "other modifications, alternatively, to achieve an equivalent result." I have done the former. – PS

This book is boring. I will admit that much. Rather, nothing has happened so far — just some backstory and an introduction to the characters. Or perhaps a few things have started to happen, but were taken off-course by a long digression about a band. Mostly, so far, it's been Ganbold's backstory, Florian's backstory. Haruko's next. The writing process was linear: I began at the start — although not necessarily the start of the story — and wrote through to the end. Then I went back and started reading the manuscript right from the beginning yet again — I'm in the process of re-reading it now for the second time — and I have to say I'm still a little disappointed with these opening chapters. Again, nothing much happens, and I doubt there is adequate suggestion of the point that is to come.

If I can defend the story so far, I might remind you of novels that begin slowly, but pick up speed. Yevgeny Zamyatin's *We* is one of those. I've read it numerous times, and each time was about to put it down before the story enlivened itself; the closing sections are quite brisk, exciting and hopeful even. It ends heroically — to an extent. I'm not sure I can say the same thing about *Naked Defiance*, but I can assure you things are going to start happening, and I do hope you will read to the conclusion. Or perhaps I needn't be concerned. Perhaps you have been satisfied with *Naked Defiance* so far, even if these opening sections are taking a while. When I am on a commuter train I often see people reading very large books — six hundred pages or more — so I think volume means a lot to some people. Merely having more words must count for something. Of course, you could just wave your hand in front of your face... But no — I think there's more here to make your reading time worthwhile.

I wrote this book to serve a purpose — as more than a pastime — and hopefully you will uncover that purpose. This book is a memoir, of sorts. And a worthwhile memoir — or any book — should have a strong point to help drive it along. If I seem unconfident this narrative has not driven you along adequately so far it is because its point, I feel, could perhaps be more pointed. Or perhaps I should have faith that you will read between the lines, as they say. You really must do so because this book has been censored. I censored it as I wrote the first draft, I censored it more during the second draft, and that perhaps softens its impact. Perhaps I was afraid, in the current environment... Well, let me just say that as an author my profile was and continues to be zero: some of my writing gets published, but usually it is ignored. I don't — now I should write, *didn't* — care to know what would happen if my profile as an author were suppressed *below zero*. Not as a man with responsibilities...

In any event, when I created this narrative the first time, when I went through this story, I censored whatever you can't have in a story in this country. I erased the names of external human sexual organs — or at least reduced the number of times they are mentioned. I also deleted any direct criticism of the government. I made sure that if there was any criticism to level in this book, it was disguised as criticism of someplace far away in time or even space — especially if, by not disguising it as such, trade sanctions might be a possible consequence. And

I've kept that largely the same. The one thing I've decided to change, however — the one place I will take a risk — is to clarify the identity of the main protagonist. Because something has changed, and revealing the identity no longer seems so risky.

Here I'll state quite plainly that the main protagonist — the narrator — is me. I'm Florian. The narrator is Florian, the author is Florian, and when I started this book — this memoir — I had reasons to disassociate myself from its content. But now I have less to lose (you'll understand this sometime later in the book), and now I can just come right out and tell you: I'm Florian, and I'm willing to submit to a genealogical DNA test to prove it — to prove this is an *authentic story*, if that's what you'd like.

Stepping back a few paces, it might be confusing to start reading a book with a "foreword" written in the first person, followed by the story itself purportedly about a different person but also in the first person — and then this. I thought not to put *this* in at all, and to hope you would overlook the false distinction I had made between the writer and the protagonist. I was also concerned you might object to what seems to be a self-consciously "postmodern" move — whatever that means. In truth, I wanted to avoid it. I thought it might seem gimmicky, or just *old fashioned*. That is, until a writer friend of mine (yes, there are other writers who associate with me) pointed out that it's just standard practice. It's been done so many times it fails to stand apart from *writing-as-usual*. So I did it, and now the reader can know I am Florian, and that should provide more clarity. The author and the protagonist are the same. There's no point in denying it. And I think it might help sell the book — though probably not. But I'm happy if more people read it, and now I don't care if they know who I am. I've taken bigger risks in my life and lost more (as you'll see).

This isn't to say, however, that this memoir is exactly a *confessional*. Another *old-fashioned* thing I've done is to write a memoir that's not entirely *biographical*. Yes, I am Florian, and yes, I am the author of this story. Nevertheless, items taken from my life have been distorted, much as a guitarist distorts a guitar sound with effects — in case you are tired of the same old naturalistic guitar sound of "reality." Robert Walser wrote: "We don't need to see anything out of the ordinary. We already see so much." Do we? Yes, I know the other way this statement can be read, but sometimes we have no idea what we're seeing — or hearing. That is, until we are surprised.

When I was fifteen years old (this is a true story) I heard, for the first time, the song "Ahead" by the band Wire, the main version as it sounds on the album *The Ideal Copy*. In this recording the guitar sounds only remotely like a guitar, and I took a liking to it. It was the first time I had heard the guitar that way. And now I am reminded that at that time I was working at a plant nursery that specialized in ground cover. My job, that spring, was to discard plants that had died during the winter. The owner of the nursery was an old German man who had seen his brother jump to his death during the firebombing of Dresden...

5

The Bridge Building, a minimalistic eleven stories, must have looked quite futuristic when it was built roughly a century ago. It was so-called for the vantage it provided of a bascule bridge, which then crossed a marsh on the inland side of a shallow inlet. The marsh was later filled in, the bridge supplanted by a highway intersection with two off-ramps, each making a 180-degree loop around the tower from opposite sides; its owners were apparently too stubborn to sell it off and allow for its demolition. Later thinking would have the highway intersection partly dismantled, its remnants repurposed as bicycle lanes. This did nothing, however, to reduce the sheer volume of car traffic, which was rerouted to other local streets. (Such was the insistence of the majority, it seemed, to use cars no matter how absurdly inefficient.)

Our next meeting would be at the Bridge Building, then the location of a number of unique businesses which could survive only in that low-rent and partly abandoned district of the city. Haruko Rusakova — formerly Agnieszka Møller, or "Aggy" for short — suggested we meet an hour ahead so that she could give a fuller recounting of her transformation. It was an unusually hot, bright day and the building and overpass remnants cast hard shadows on one another. I walked down one curved overpass to a darkened skyway to the third floor. One could hardly imagine the change from outside to inside: a shop selling other kinds of remnant, and in fact called Remnants. There I found Haruko — I knew I mustn't call her Agnieszka or Aggy — pondering a shelf of blown-glass objects, patterned with bright swirls of colour.

"I can recognize the skill required to make these," she said, "but I don't like them at all. These aren't cheap things, but they cheapen the shop."

"I think I understand what you mean."

"It's as if they're running out of the past. Or maybe they're too lazy. But no — I really do think the past is just slipping away."

"I was here with my son, once. He found an Armin Trösser manual coffee grinder — young children are fascinated by simple machines. I picked it up because I drink coffee, but I had no idea at the time —"

"A burr mill. They were made in Germany and West Germany anytime between the 1930s and 1950s, although I have no idea when mine was made — I have one, too. It's quite hard to find accurate details."

"They're made of beech, and of course I wonder where the tree was felled, who finished and assembled the pieces, and where and when."

"During the Third Reich."

"Maybe."

"You'd think there would be a record, somewhere. It makes you wonder. But these —" she said, motioning to the blown-glass objects, "they don't."

"I agree. But what can they do if all the things of the past have just vanished?"

"It's simply too bad, because I used to like this place a lot more."

Against one wall was an immense chest of very small drawers and we examined their interiors, which contained variously a Baculites fossil from the Burgess Shale, the gear shift knob for a 1976 Nissan Violet, a Praktica EE2 camera body, *sueki* pottery fragments, various glass insulators...

"I chose 'Haruko' because that was my great-great grand-mother's name."

"In Denmark?"

"Well, yes. There has never been much of a Japanese population in Denmark, as you might expect. Either she was attached to a Japanese delegation to Denmark in 1873, or she was named after someone attached to that delegation. In any event, it seems my great-great grandfather was some kind of trade bureaucrat.

The family records disappeared when my grandmother's house burned down. It was a kitchen fire. She survived the fire, but didn't live long after that. Should I get a genealogical DNA test? My previous name was chosen by my mother, who is French but her family immigrated from Poland."

"I'm sorry I didn't recognize you at first, but it's not just your name that has changed —"

"I look old. I look older."

"We all look older. It's been about fifteen years. But I wouldn't say you look old. In fact, when I saw you at the beach, I thought you looked quite youthful, that you could be a much younger woman. And up close, too."

"There isn't much substance for gravity. I knew who you were right away, though. Your eyes haven't changed."

"Now that I know you were 'Aggy'... I can see her face. But you do seem like a different person."

"Yes. I had to get beyond that time, and I did. I had to change everything to feel completely free from it."

"I hope it wasn't your experience with Rondo X."

"Of course not. You were among the first nice young men I met. You were older than me, but you were still young men, and I was younger still — just a child. Well, my father was a man. He was a good person, so perhaps it shouldn't have surprised me that you were good people, too. But somehow, all the other men in my life until... all the young men in my life until then —"

"You used the past tense for your father."

"He passed away."

"I'm sorry."

"Not at all. It has been quite some years now. I'm glad he got to know me as 'Haruko' while he was alive. I think it meant a lot to him that I took my name from his side of the family. Anyway, for some reason... I don't know why I associated with young men who were… just idiots, frankly. I still can't figure it out. Then I met you, and Marc, and Gerrit… and what's the other one's name?"

"Rubin."

"Right. Well, you were so different from the other young men I had known. You were polite, respectful. You asked for my ideas. You didn't leer at me. You didn't make me feel like a tool or some object to be passed around. You were just… decent."

"To be fair, every man — every person has the potential to be foolish, to be cruel. I know I have been at times in my life."

"So have I. But no — you were all very different from the young men I had known until then. I met you at most a dozen times. But even in that short amount of time it was clear. It was a revelation."

I was a precocious child, Haruko continued. All of those things one would expect of a girl from an aspirant bourgeois family — I did them. Ballet, piano, good grades at school… Funnily enough, neither of my parents encouraged me — not particularly. In fact I begged my parents to let me try this, that, and the other thing. Whatever I saw my childhood friends doing, I wanted to try. At first it was out of curiosity, then competitively. I wasn't overtly competitive, but I did want to be the best, and I did do very, very well. When I was twelve I starred in our school's production of *Annie*, and I was Clara in a local production of *The Nutcracker*. I sang in the school choir, composed my own songs for talent contests, won top student awards. Success followed success.

At the age of fifteen, however, things rapidly changed. I was starting to get a picture of the wider world. I was very good at many things, but was a prodigy at none. I might be good enough for *The Nutcracker* in my own city, I might earn some money acting in television commercials (which I did on two occasions), I would certainly get some scholarships for music… but it would be very hard to be at the top. I mean the very top, which is what I wanted. I was used to hard work, but my obsessiveness started to wane. I was burned out, really. And I saw other young people having what seemed to me a lot more fun. If I can put it down to one event, I think it was an overnight ski excursion I signed up for at a local community centre. To make a long story short, I got drunk for the very first time. Another girl on the trip had somehow smuggled a twelve-pack of coolers. Well, soon we were hanging out again. She introduced me to other girls and boys of her ilk. On weekends we would hover around liquor stores with cash in hand, asking adults to bootleg for us, and many did. Some of us could pass as adults, but mostly we had to ask someone who had legitimate ID. Unless one of us had fake ID. We were also smoking lots of pot, often ending up at the country house of Tommy, whose parents — his dad was a veterinarian — always seemed to be away on weekends.

My parents were extremely slow to catch on to what was happening to me. If I quit this and that, the excuse was that I needed to get more focussed on school, to make sure I had top grades for university. When I was out on weekends, they willingly provided spending money, which they were told was for snacks. More often than not, it was to buy drive-through marijuana. Someone at a local fast-food restaurant had opened a side business: the code was to ask for "an extra eighth cheese" on your hamburger when purchasing at the drive-through window. Shawna, who I met on the ski trip, was a year older than me and had a driver's license. She was the one who always picked me up at my parents' house. She looked very respectable.

She was also an honour roll student, and my parents hadn't a clue what we were up to.

Someone they never met, though, was Tommy. Even though we soon started "dating," if you want to call it that. He was tall and looked older for his age and for those reasons, I think, had an easy way with girls. Now I'd see a guy like Tommy as "just some idiot in a rasta hat." It was a very unfortunate first love, if I concede having had no idea of love. I was drunk, we were drunk all the time. I learned — I was told, because he was the one with experience — that sex was just for fun. It was sport. Simple physical stimulation. I don't want to relive these memories in detail, but let me just say I didn't feel respected. In the following years it crossed my mind to join one of those cults that promised reclaimed virginity.

It gets worse because soon enough we were on to cocaine, and credit card fraud. Tommy was an expert at fake ID and he soon moved up to credit card theft, buying high priced items, reselling them, and using the cash for drugs. I ended up helping him with this. I admit there was something thrilling about it. But I also knew I was just being used. I was barely keeping up appearances at school and at home. I was burning myself out again, in a different way. It wasn't until I was charged and convicted as a youth offender, and put under house arrest with an ankle bracelet for two months, that I finally realized the extent of my utter failure. And then my parents understood, too. I was just seventeen, almost eighteen when this happened.

Being under house arrest gave me time to think, to dry out and get healthy again. I was depressed. My mother was depressed. She wanted to help me, but was distant. She was in shock for a long time after that. It was hard for her to reconcile the Agnieszka she had raised with the one I had become, and it was just as hard for me. For a former perfectionist, the downfall was hard to take — but I wanted to fix my mistakes and move on. My father, thankfully, was especially understanding and supportive at that time. He had become a father late in life and was near retirement. As the child of parents who had lived through the Depression, he inherited their thriftiness and long-range thinking, and had already saved quite a bit by the time I had my crisis. To support me, his only child, he went part-time for the remainder of his career and made himself available to me as a kind of coach, helping me keep a schedule, plan, and stay in good health. He advised me to return to my erstwhile creative pursuits — music in particular. He had connections, so I got occasional jobs as a studio backing vocalist. And this is how I ended up performing on that song of yours.

By the time you met me, I was almost twenty. I looked very healthy, and I was organized. If I was hurting inside, it may not have occurred to you. That is, unless you recognized my strong work ethic as that of a former drug user trying to keep busy and distracted. Indeed, I was still in distress, struggling to overcome the shock of what had happened. I was always being reminded; when I enrolled in adult education to earn my secondary school graduation certificate, then in university classes in which most other students were two or three years younger than me, or when I worried that someone would recognize me as Aggy — *that* Aggy.

Ultimately — to make a complete transformation and move beyond those events that had derailed my life — I would need to change even my name. Which is how Agnieszka "Aggy" Møller became Haruko Møller. And when I was twenty-seven I met Dmitry Rusakov, a beautiful man with striking green eyes, studious in his particularly Russian way: he has a degree in architecture, can speak five languages, and trained to be an aircraft mechanic out of sheer personal interest. Being some years older than me, by the time I met him he was wise with the experience of age (whereas my wisdom arose from a particular psychic turmoil). He is gentle and kind, and I have him to thank too for the utter transformation in my life. Well, perhaps I can thank myself, too: experience gave me the wisdom to recognize I was being loved in return, that I had met someone with whom I could spend my life. So we married, and I took his name — not because I feel a woman needs to take her husband's name, but simply because I can. That is how I became Haruko Rusakova.

6

We assembled for the meeting at Bridge Books, also in the Bridge Building. Haruko and I took the ancient elevator. It may have been faster to take the stairs — the bookstore was just two floors down — but we were tempted by the novelty of an ancient elevator with manual doors. Bridge Books itself was also a novelty. It wasn't a large store, perhaps no larger than a two-bedroom apartment, and seemed designed to be reconfigured as such. It had its own washroom — just a toilet and sink, although no bath or shower — and a very small galley kitchen with a serving window, from which one could order a very small number of items, or perhaps just two: garlic toast and tea. There was an open seating area with various folding chairs and tables. Curtains were drawn across the large glass pane in the upper third of the shop's entrance door. There was also a sign announcing the shop's closure for an "event rental." The event was our Defiance meeting, and the space was not in fact rented: the pair who owned Bridge Books were also Defiance members.

Haruko and I were somewhat early, and spent some time browsing the books, most of which were used, many of which were rare — although I was not qualified to assess their exchange value, which to me seemed intangible, esoteric. There was a well-preserved copy of Wilhelm Fraenger's *Hieronymus Bosch*, printed in the German Democratic Republic. I was tempted to buy it. *The Life of Vasilii Kandinsky in Russian Art*, edited by John E. Bowlt, with a slightly torn dust jacket. *An Illustrated History of Seaplanes and Flying Boats* by Maurice F. Allward.

Hitler: A Study in Tyranny by Alan Bullock. *Duran Duran* by Neil Gaiman. *The Observer's Book of Sea Fishes* by Lawrence Wells. *The Observer's Book of Automobiles* (1967) by L.A. Manwaring. *A Cavalier History of Surrealism* by Raoul Vaneigem. *Bradshaw's Canals and Navigable Rivers of England and Wales* by H. R. De Salis. A cheap paperback version of *To the Lighthouse* by Virginia Woolf. I had a quick look at all of these books.

———————

We discussed our most recent actions — those following the meeting at Ganbold's house. Haruko's envelope had indicated not only a date, but also that her action would require a full day. She had obviously been willing to accept the challenge, nevertheless surprised by the complexity of the instructions. Four performers were required. One was to transport the other three by car — it was a blue 1985 Toyota TownAce, by Haruko's recollection — and to port changes of clothing to the performance end-point.

Haruko was taken to the north end of a coastal trail that had been designed as an evacuation route for the survivors of shipwrecks. There, she changed into her costume: merely a *fundoshi* and a *Noh*-style mask. She had to create her own *fundoshi*, but the mask was supplied — the driver came with a box full of masks, Haruko told me. She chose an expressionless, feminine mask. She also had to paint herself fully with a chalky white makeup. The driver assisted by ensuring the makeup was evenly distributed across her back.

Alone, Haruko began her journey south at low tide along the rocky coast, along a trail that was mostly up from the water through a bright forest of fir trees hung with beard lichens. The trail had been cut through tall salal, which dominated the forest floor. The instructions were for her to walk slowly and mindfully, to "appreciate the sensation of each step," to make digressions from the pathway in order to seek the following plants and animals: skunk cabbage, sitka valerian, saxifrage; chitons, sea anemones, sea urchins. When each was found, she was to attempt "telepathic communication." She spent the most time, she told me, with one chiton, then another, which despite their articulated shells showed no signs of ever having moved. ("More than anything, I wanted to see them move," she said.) The mask eliminated her peripheral vision. This was alternately frightening, alternately helpful to focussing on the task.

"It was gruelling, really," she said. "It must have been at least three hours before I heard the other two — before I saw them arrive from the other direction. One had a bright red robe of some kind of light, shiny material. The other had the same in blue. That's all they were wearing of course. And their *Noh* masks — one like a demon, the other like an old man. One was swinging an incense burner like the kind you'd see at a Catholic church — a thurible, I think it's called. The other was shaking some sleigh bells on bracelets. When we met we were to sit down, face the ocean, and improvise a chant. I was cold — almost shivering cold — dehydrated, hungry, exhausted... I started laughing. Hysterically. We all started laughing, and I think it was all for the same reason. It felt absurd. It felt like someone had played a joke on us."

"Did anyone see you?"

"I'm not sure. The only people I noticed were a family. A man and a woman with a young child, perhaps eight or nine years old. All in their hiking boots and windbreakers: it was a fairly cool, grey day — although the sun had appeared now and again. Anyway, they kept their distance. By the time we got changed — the driver eventually came with our clothes — we looked just as normal as they did, I'm sure. Was your action nearly as elaborate?"

"No. All I had to do was visit a kind of home goods kiosk in a train station. I had to look for the display version of a specific desk lamp — one with a flexible neck. I had to pick it up, inspect it visually, weigh it with my hands, test its functions. While still holding it, I was to close my eyes for 'about one minute' according to the instructions and 'meditate on its inner sound.'"

"Do you think anyone noticed?"

"I believe so."

"It's certainly a contrast in labour."

———————————————

Ganbold was among the first, after Haruko and me, to arrive at the meeting. We spoke briefly, and he was soon joined by the nude from the last party, who took most of his attention from that point on. She introduced herself as Foreste, spelling her name for us, explaining it was in fact the name chosen by her parents. She was more affable, less aloof, and less exclusive than she had appeared to be from a distance. She was the only one unclothed at that point. As she was standing near me, I thought I would be distracted by her nudity, but hardly noticed — such was her total engagement in the conversation.

Many more went straight to Ganbold as they entered the shop, or to Sarah (Engels, according to her business card), one of the shop's owners. The turnout was similar to that of the prior meeting — about two dozen. After this critical mass had been achieved, Sarah — I can describe her only as a woman of a certain age, the unsmiling yet gentle essence of sincerity and organization — took the role as meeting chair, and reminded us of our mission.

We began by debriefing our most recent actions. Aside from that of Haruko's group, all had been performed solo. One set of instructions required the actor to fill a small jar with one-centimetre twig segments, then attempt to exchange them for "a product of equal value" at an electronics shop. Another set of instructions was simply this: "nothing can have value, without being an object of utility. If the thing is useless, so is the labour contained in it; the labour does not count as labour and therefore creates no value."

"I recognize that from Marx, *Capital*," said Sarah.

"What did you do?" asked Ganbold.

"It was a problem," said the actor. She was sitting cross-legged on the floor, warming her hands with a mug of tea; a young woman with long, sandy-coloured hair who wore a shawl, but nothing else. (She was surreptitiously naked, somehow a distraction compared to Foreste's simple nudity.) "I'm embarrassed to say I couldn't come up with a very creative solution. I went to a busy shopping street and waved at no one."

"I was arrested," said another actor. He was standing, leaning against the door frame to the next room, also with a cup of tea; a man of about thirty with a curly black beard, curly untrimmed hair everywhere, rimless spectacles, but nothing else.

The revelation (of the arrest) turned some heads. Ganbold looked concerned. Referring to the man by his name — Lou — he asked why he had been arrested.

"It was the so-called no-pants subway ride," he said. "My instructions were to attend the ride and actually take off my pants, so I did."

"And I take it you weren't wearing anything underneath," said Ganbold.

"Exactly."

"Well, I'm sorry this happened. You know, we're not supposed to create actions that may get our comrades here into any trouble."

"I didn't really mind, you know." (This was clear: in contrast to the woman in the shawl, there was nothing surreptitious about Lou's nakedness.) "I'm not a big fan of those 'flash mob' style events," he continued. "No, they really annoy me and I'm having trouble articulating why, aside from their obvious part in the spectacle, and their obvious lack of courage. I mean, if they say no pants, they should really mean no pants. I was happy to disrupt it."

"What about the police?"

"Well, I should clarify, I'm not sure I was officially arrested. They just said to me, 'put your pants on' and I said, 'but this is the no-pants subway ride,' and they went straight to the handcuffs and hauled me off the train, so I put my pants back on and they gave me a warning."

Then a new speaker: "Men's parts are still controversial." It was a woman — not old, but with noticeable grey in her dark, wavy hair. She was thin — not a malnourished skinny, but wiry, although not like a distance runner: she appeared to be someone who, by their nature, simply consumes a lot of energy. She was seated with her back to the wall, wearing nothing but, curiously, knee-high socks — those kind of very typical grey work socks. "I wonder if they would have come down so hard on you — or even noticed — if you had been a woman. Or maybe they would have noticed, in a different way —"

"That's a valid point," said Ganbold. "But I think we need to discuss how disruptive we're willing to be. When our actions cross over and become simply part of the spectacle."

"I think we should," said the thin one. Her tone was still what one might call congenial, but there was an element of challenge in it, too — an abruptness, suggesting she hadn't liked being cut off.

————————

Here the discussion became to a certain extent contentious. Its intensity never increased to the brazenness of an argument — not the kind that one side insisted on winning — but it was clear there were some unresolved questions about the aims of Defiance. Ganbold spoke at length of the choreographic nature of the group's actions, referring on numerous occasions to "choreographic notations," emphasizing that the performance should always be, for the actor, esoteric. We should be completely at one with the performance, "bonded to it in an oceanic way," he said. Doing so "intensifies its authenticity" for the unwitting audience. No one disagreed. The main question, rather, was how overt or confrontational these performances should be.

The thin one — whose name, I learned through the debate, was Solomiya — reminded us that our purpose was "not just experiential, but oppositional." Someone asked — they clarified it was not a rhetorical question — how we can affect change while not being seen, how we can challenge the spectacle of capitalism without making, to some extent, a spectacle. Ganbold reminded us that if the performances are even seen — they might not in fact be seen—that it is sufficient if they bring "delight, mystery, surprise or any combination" to an audience accustomed to "the miserable logic of capitalism."

Solomiya spoke up again, asking us to consider the audience's "mindless complicity" in that logic. "I'd like to do more to challenge it," she said. "As they further erode anyone's access to authentic life, there needs to be more push-back." We can do that, said Ganbold, if we "embody the alternative" and "help them see." Solomiya countered that "mindless practitioners of the current system are unable to see — unless we rub it right in their faces. We need to disturb them. Make them feel disturbed." They need to take responsibility, she said, "to make reparations for the destruction they have wrought on the human mind."

The discussion was mostly between Ganbold and Solomiya, apart from one notable interjection: "This reminds me of the Ohno/Hijikata duality in *butoh*." It was a man, clothed, who looked quite stereotypically like a fashion model — not someone with discrete knowledge of a dance form that, among other things, confronted received notions of beauty. And yet he went on at length. It was somewhat disarming.

The mood lightened and here the woman in the shawl suggested, playfully, "Since we're all clearly anti-miserablist, and because I think we want to intensify things a bit — at least here at these meetings — why don't we all be naked?"

"That would probably be in order," said the fashion model. "John Berger writes..." Here he grabbed a copy of Berger's *Ways of Seeing* — there were five copies in total, on a nearby bookshelf — and started flipping through the pages.

"That's a book I highly recommend," interjected Sarah, the shop owner.

"Berger writes, 'To be naked is to be oneself.' "

"Yes, but what are the next two sentences?" asked Ganbold.

"Let's see... 'To be nude is to be seen naked by others and yet not recognized for oneself. A naked body has to be seen as an object in order to become a nude.' "

"Yes, and I think a bit further down the page he writes something to the effect, 'nudity is a form of dress' — if those aren't his exact words. In performance, anyway, I think we need to be cautious about how we use our nudity, or our nakedness. Although here, at these meetings, being naked is certainly apropos."

"It means we can be ourselves," said the one in the shawl, "and not be objects, which is what we're after."

"I'm all for it," said Lou. "Just as long as we start calling ourselves Naked Defiance."

"Well, if that's what everyone wants," said Ganbold, "why not?"

Here there was a strong feeling this was truly what the meeting wanted. Sometimes one can feel this kind of momentum, and there's no need to define it explicitly. Ganbold was nevertheless inscrutable, and I wondered if he too was taken up by the will of the meeting, or voicing his support simply in order to stay within the "opinion corridor" — so as not to diminish his authority in the group.

In short order the clothes came off. Our clothes came off. This was a relief, in two senses: I no longer needed to think about whether to be clothed or unclothed, nor did I have to worry about my wardrobe (which had little variety due to budgetary constraints, especially since having children). At the same time, the requirement for nudity might raise other concerns. Bridge Books was a small space, which made it hard not to brush against others as we manoeuvred to find open space on the bookshelves for our garments — although, if we did brush against one another, no one appeared to take offence. And I needed to take care not to comment on the others' nudity with my gaze. I wouldn't do so intentionally, not in speech, certainly, but Haruko — now standing right in front of me, this was the first time I had seen her with her clothes off this close up — was not so circumspect. "In any event," she said, motioning to Ganbold, "he has nothing to worry about. He's quite pristine for his age."

"What about the conversation?" I asked, changing the topic. "About the mandate. Is that usual?" I was surprised things seemed to have changed so quickly at just my second meeting.

"I agree with what Solomiya said. I think I agree with it — mostly. I think we should do more."

7

What Aïsha would have thought of Defiance — now Naked Defiance — I am not sure. She had a general idea of our mandate. It might not have interested her, personally, but she's the one who encouraged me to get involved. We had been together almost fifteen years and over that period — especially since my wasted attempt to revive an erstwhile top-20 hit (number 20, exactly) on the Netherlands pop charts — I had been fully devoted to our family. Virtually everything I did was centred on providing stability: establishing my career as a warehouse manager, saving any surplus income, socializing our children. Unlike Aïsha, I had done this to the exclusion of almost all else. Between the time our son, Travel, had begun to walk and the time he began to ask "why" at every opportunity (I would say this is when a man can finally start to feel more useful as a parent) I had not created a thing. I had no hobbies. And our daughter, Trudi, was just two years behind. During this busy time Aïsha had nevertheless retained her connection to sound, occasionally dusting off gear to reconnect with old music friends. She was quite disciplined about making her own time for this, and was perplexed that I hadn't maintained at least some connections through music or art in general. And once Travel and Trudi were in school, which provided me some extra time, there really was no excuse. Aïsha told me to I had to start doing something again — that my subscription to *Wallpaper** magazine wasn't good enough ("You hate it, anyway," she said) and that I actually had to start making something again. That was my impetus.

When two people are attracted to each other — very attracted to each other — there's no need to think twice. The thing — the attraction — must only be accepted. Aïsha's naturally curly hair — I had never been with a woman with hair of such quality; I imagined weighing it in my hands. Her eyes and voice. The sound of the Roland TR-808, which I sold to her. The lesson I gave explaining its functions because I had lost the instruction manual. Her hair, the intensity of her gaze as she leaned over the machine. Her voice. Her first test pattern. Electric snare and open hi-hat. Adjusting the snare pitch. Sakura blossoms just outside the window of my second-storey apartment built in the early 1960s. Chrome V-shaped drawer handles. Parquet floor. It comes back to me like an instantaneous cubist image; synesthetic sound-colour. And the next day, too. She called me and said there was something she hadn't been able to figure out.

"I want to know what these buttons do. This one."

"Which?" I asked.

"It'll be easier to see if you come over here."

She had the machine set up on the kitchen table and was standing next to it.

"I want to know this," she said as she manoeuvred herself closer to me, angled the TR-808 toward to me. Leaning over the machine — we were both leaning toward the machine as she indicated a button I thought would have a very obvious function — she turned her face toward me, and I faced her because I thought maybe... and I could feel... and she was now much closer to me than someone merely enquiring...

The TR-808 is now in a display case in our living room. In the same case is a square fiddle made by Aïsha's great uncle (her grandmother's brother), and two copper candle holders which belonged to my great grandparents (the parents of my grandmother on my father's side). Each holder is etched with an intricate pattern, subtly different from that of the other. I am told they were made in the 1920s, although I have no way to verify that, or where they were made and whether they were the product of factory work. The fiddle is of course unique, and we know exactly who made it, and the approximate year in which it was made — either 1973 or 1974, according to a record of the maker's work, which was regionally famous. As for the TR-808, we know it was designed by a team of engineers employed by the Roland Corporation in Japan. On our tenth wedding anniversary, Aïsha and I wrote a letter to Kakehashi Ikutaro, founder of the Roland Corporation, expressing our gratitude for the machine that brought us together. In return, we received a congratulatory note from his secretary, and we have framed it and placed it beside the TR-808.

The TR-808 snare sound is but a variation of a burst of static. It is not the sound of a snare drum, but *stands for* the sound of a snare drum. One could say that any recording of a snare sound is merely a representation or a signifier of the thing itself. Of course the TR-808 snare is not a recording or a sample, but a synthetic simulation. We identify it as a snare sound only as it relates to the other sounds — bass drum, tom drum, closed hi-hat, crash cymbal, etc. — that comprise what we know to be a drum kit. It is not a snare drum or a naturalistic snare drum sound, but rather a representation of that sound and also a signifier for the future. Just as when we hear the word "tree" and an image of a tree arrives in our minds (even if it is not the same tree for each one of us), when we hear the TR-808 we automatically consider the future — such is the machine's ubiquity in future sounds. Thus, when we hear the opening to Simple Minds' "New Gold Dream (81-82-83-84)," we automatically consider a point in the future, even though the numbers identify dates in the past. (I should add, however, that it was in fact a predecessor to the TR-808 — a machine from Roland's CompuRhythm series — that was used.)

Now the TR-808 in our display case stands for us — for Aïsha and Florian, and the life we made together, and our children Travel and Trudi. Yes, that is the reason their names start "Tr." They are our legacy. Likewise, our TR-808 will outlast us, and will carry us into the future. It contains rhythms programmed by Aïsha and me. It contains something of us and one might say it is a cybernetic extension of our minds, and of our mind together. It is a reification.

I occasionally wonder if it is right that our relationships are mediated by things, or perhaps by commodities. I remember Ganbold saying something to this effect: "Let us remember these performances are not bereft of commodities and the spectacle just to surprise others, but also to surprise ourselves, to bring us closer to authentic, unmediated experience." But our display case... a container of magic... a container of necromancy... is it not also an authentic, unmediated relationship? My ideas sometimes get muddled. Yet this thing... the thing that makes my life with Aïsha concrete... is not something I need to think about twice.

8

I was shopping for food — which is something one must do, unless one grows one's own. It was a small supermarket in my neighbourhood. Not a large, gleaming supermarket, but a small one — rusticated. It had a floor of broad, wood planks. Lots of green and brown. A section for products indicated as "local" and "organic." A delicatessen area with hardly any self-serve — one was compelled in most cases to order from a clerk. Located on the ground floor of a concrete tower, and with all the products of multinational industry one might find elsewhere, this supermarket had nevertheless been modelled as a *country market*. It was the spectacle of a country market. If I were being honest with myself, I would say I shopped there because it shielded me from reality more and frightened me less than a large, gleaming supermarket that makes no pretense: we are ripping fish from the sea as quickly as we can, none of this food is truly natural. Or let me be even more honest: I was taking a *professional interest*. I couldn't help it. I was the manager of a natural foods warehouse. I wanted to know if they were stocking our wares, giving them shelf prominence, moving units.

I rounded a corner and entered the aisle for cereals, grains, baking supplies. (We had recently started handling a new brand, "Papa Natural's." Could I find the bearded mascot?) There I found Solomiya, in conversation with another woman — younger, not ectomorphic. The first thing I noticed was her lipstick, somewhere between red and pink — a shade chosen perhaps for its "3-D" effect against her light complexion. She wore tennis shoes and a light dress with an oversized, gaudy floral pattern. Solomiya and I made eye contact — long enough that I felt compelled to speak.

"Solomiya?"

"Yes, that's right. Actually, Solomiya." (She emphasized the second syllable.) We met each other at the meeting, didn't we? But I'm sorry I didn't catch your name."

"Florian. Florian Moore."

"Good to see you again. Solomiya Gura. And this is Erika."

"Erika Kaiser. Pleased to meet you," said the one with the bright lipstick. She curtsied and held out her hand. (It felt moist, and this somehow brought me to a synesthetic realization — that Erika was an emissary of the natural world; the essence of steam rising from a quickly heating rainforest.)

"Erika used to come to our Defiance meetings," said Solomiya.

"That's right. I used to. Yes. Well, sorry I have to run. You know, it's about time for my appointment," said Erika. "It was nice meeting you, Florian. And good to run into you again, Solomiya. We should catch up again."

"Absolutely," said Solomiya. "I'd like to know more about what you've been up to, creatively."

"Too-da-loo!" (There was something nervous yet at the same time sarcastic in the way she said this.)

Erika now away, Solomiya continued, "We weren't radical enough for her, that's for sure."

"She seems like someone who wants to make a statement," I suggested.

"Indeed. And she's continued with her own actions, which she calls 'surprises.' But there were other things, too."

"Oh?"

"Oh yes. You should have seen it. She really butted heads with Ganbold, was put off by him in particular."

"Why?"

"Well, you haven't seen that side of him, because this all happened before you got involved. But the things he used to say at those meetings... It really irked a lot of people — some of the women in particular, although not all of them, evidently."

"Like what?"

"Well, there was always this edge of prurience. It was hard to put a finger on it, but there was always something suggestive in what he'd say. Every so often a phrase would enter his speech — *the power to vivify, depths of one's self, presence of the spiritual, the spirit penetrates matter, the life force appears where there is a void* — and you'd wonder what he was really talking about. It *felt* quite brazen — but was hard to put a finger on, at the same time."

"I didn't know there was that side of him."

"You wouldn't, because he's toned it down lately. Quite a bit."

"Those phrases — it all sounds like Gurdjieff."

"Exactly. Obscenely suggestive — or suggestively obscene. With a dose of snake oil. I must admit I was somehow drawn in by his words: he conveyed them with such conviction, and yet… my reflex was to push away, to feel I was being manipulated. Not that I feel that way anymore. He hardly ever says the kind of thing he used to say — maybe not at all. He had moved on from that, even when Erika was still around. So, like me, she might have stayed involved — but she got spooked."

"By what?"

"She was out on an action — out in the middle of nowhere — and ended up being chased for quite some time by a man with a horse mask. She wasn't sure if it was supposed to be part of the action — there was nothing on the instruction card to indicate it should have been — but she got the impression the man knew. That somehow he knew she would be there. She came to the next meeting and told us all about it. She was in tears. Some of us were in disbelief. Ganbold was impassive, said nothing, was impossible to read. And she never came back, although I've stayed in touch with her outside of Defiance. Other strange things have happened, too."

"Oh?"

"Yes. A few other strange things. I was about to go look for some jam."

"So was I. Marmalade. I'm heading in the same direction."

———————————

When Solomiya and I rounded the corner into the next aisle we found Erika at the far end, sitting on the floor, in conversation with the store's manager. In keeping with the store's image he had a moustache and wore an apron.

"What are you doing?" he asked.

"You tell me. What am I doing?"

"Can you please leave the store?"

"But you haven't answered my question. What am I doing?"

"You know very well what you're doing." (He described what she was doing. I must have blushed.)

"You know, you shouldn't talk that way to a lady."

"Whatever. Maybe you should try acting like a lady."

"Do you have something against what I'm doing here with… What is this stuff?" She looked at the open jar and read the label: "'Papa Natural's Concentrated Oat Cream.'"

(This certainly jarred me. Somehow I took it personally — although I shouldn't have.)

"No. Of course I don't have anything against it. Just that you're doing it in my store. Did you pay for it?"

"What?"

"That stuff. The stuff you're doing that with."

"Oh. This stuff. Can't people just make it at home? Why does it need to be all packaged up in plastic? What's it good for, anyway?"

(Well, some people are quite busy, you know. Plastic packaging is lighter and therefore requires less fuel to transport than glass.

The oat cream tastes better than what most people can make on their own. And it's good for your skin, too.)

"Tell me, do you see women's bodies as just one more commodity to be bought and sold?"

"What does that have to do with anything? Of course not."

"What about oat milk?"

"Can you just leave, please? Look at what you're doing! There are children in here."

"Then someone should have been wearing protection!"

At this point the store manager started walking away. "I'm calling the cops," he said.

"You do that! Meanwhile, I'll explore the magical relationship between commodities!" she called after him. "I'm introducing one commodity to another. I'm sure my skin is going to feel a lot smoother after this."

(That's right!)

Then in a louder voice she proclaimed: "I'm exploring the natural essence of this 'one hundred percent natural' product. I no longer wish to be alienated from it — not by a plastic jar, not by anything! Do you hear me?"

As we watched this performance from a distance, Solomiya turned to me and said, "That's going a bit far, I think. She's really lost her touch... since that incident. It must have been extremely frightening, and people react in all sorts of different ways to their emotional wounds. Some withdraw. But not Erika. She hasn't been the same person."

Erika noticed us watching and yelled down the aisle, "Hello Solomiya! Hello Florian!"

9

Following the meeting at Bridge Books, the action I had been assigned was as follows: "Go somewhere you would not usually be seen and be someone else for about an hour." It was very open ended. Being "someone else" contained infinite possibilities. How different should this person be from myself? Perhaps the most obvious possibility would be someone very, very different.

I have seen men, usually men, driving large pickup trucks — not working trucks, just big trucks, four-wheel drive, big for their own sake, noisy for their own sake, preferably diesel, with a masculine sounding name like "Ram" or "Titan," and often with something added: an ATV in the back, a jet ski on a trailer, a camping trailer roughly the same size as the apartment in which Aïsha and I were raising our family. Certainly if one of these people encountered me parking my truck at the side of a logging road, riding my ATV in the backwoods — certainly it would give them an uncanny feeling. It would be clear to them, if they were thinking at all, I thought, that I was not one of them. It would be just the kind of unsettling quotidian surprise that Ganbold had encouraged us to pursue. Seeing me unloading my ATV down a ramp from the bed of my truck — "Hey, buddy," I would say, or simply nod with an aloof sort of camaraderie — surely they would know I was not the real thing; that I might look like them, but that I was not the same thing inside. Like a raccoon meeting a tanuki. Each has the same markings: a greyish coat, dark patches around the eyes, ringed tail. From a distance they might look the same, but they are different. The raccoon belongs to the procyonid family, which includes kinkajous and cacomistles. The tanuki is a dog. They are substantially different.

Ultimately, I was deterred by the cost of renting a truck and an ATV, so instead visited a certain nature trail that my family had used as a preliminary rest stop while on road trips. There we had always stayed on the trail. But this time, at a bridge crossing a stream, I would leave the trail and follow the stream as long as I could. This was very much unlike me, I thought, to deviate from the path. It had been years, anyway, since I had made my own path in the woods. Perhaps someone would encounter me doing so here — or perhaps not. The water was lined with salmonberry bushes in bloom, and a plant called Pacific bleeding heart, which has leaves like those of carrots, and pod-like flowers that when opened resemble their name given by children: "ladies in a bath-tub." I was enchanted by sunlight glinting off the surface of the stream and minnows darting among rocks under its surface. I had intended to follow this course of water for at least the amount of time indicated by the action. After perhaps twenty minutes, however, I could go no farther. I arrived at a grate at the end of a pipe underneath a road.

Although my action at the forest stream was abbreviated, I was late getting home. Travel had an after-school guitar lesson, I had agreed to pick him up — until now it had always been his mother — but it was not to be. Traffic was heavy. I called ahead, and Aïsha did the job as usual.

Nothing seemed amiss that evening, but after the children were in bed, Aïsha told me how upset Travel had been not to see me there. He had wanted me to meet his teacher, whom he had told about his "musician" dad. "I don't think you understand how much he looks up to you," she said. But I did. He would play my old band tapes, sometimes to my embarrassment, although I didn't always mind reliving past glories. I could see he was trying hard to learn the guitar at a very young age, with little help from me. It wasn't that I minded teaching him a few things, although I didn't want to be one of those parents who pushes their children into things. And it's good, I think, to learn from more than one teacher. I let him know how proud it made me to see him choose something he wanted to learn, then take the incentive to do it. If I had any reservations, it was that I've never expected — or wanted — anyone to emulate me. Perhaps Travel could sense this, even if I never said so directly. My hope was that he'd break his own path. But who was I to judge? Maybe this was his own path. I don't know.

Well, I was alone in my office the next morning, double checking the accounts receivable, when I turned on the radio just to relieve the tedium. I always had it tuned to the local "adult-oriented rock" station — mainly because the signal from the local college station wasn't strong enough to reach the middle of the warehouse, but also because the music was largely tolerable. Whenever it wasn't, I'd just switch it off. This happened, I'd say, about five percent of the time. And what should come on first but one of my "five percent" songs: "Cat's in the Cradle" by Harry Chapin. This time, however, I decided to give it a listen. Sometimes, when I encounter something I don't like, if I'm being charitable or open-minded, I think: someone likes this, so they must have their reasons, and I can try to imagine…

Until then I'd never considered "Cat's in the Cradle" very deeply because it was exactly the kind of song I'd been dismissing since my youth. Sappy, nostalgic. Consumer capitalism manufactures nostalgia, doesn't it? Outright fascists thrive on it. And it's not "edgy" at all. That's an understatement. If I can't imagine Joy Division or Cabaret Voltaire doing their own version — or even Bryan Ferry (think: "In Every Dream Home a Heartache") — then it couldn't be any good, could it? And it's fake, too, surely. About a dad who doesn't give enough time to his son. What did Harry Chapin know about being a dad? And yet, because I was feeling charitable, I felt myself being drawn in by the song, getting "emotional," even. I was thinking about Travel and me, and Travel's guitar lesson and wanting to be close to his dad. Well, maybe Chapin did know something about being a dad. Perhaps Chapin had been driven by an impulse other than to manipulate his audience...

As I was contemplating these things — I was quite hypnotised by these thoughts, really — perhaps another song had gone by, some advertisements certainly. I was only gradually coming back to consciousness. Starting to come back to myself. I wondered: could I really have been thinking those things? And then I started hearing the DJ in traces. "... just moments ago... by now you've heard... we'll keep you informed... this very sad news... embassy officials... our hearts go out to the victims..." I couldn't catch it all because I was still contemplating...

I had no idea what the news was about — I never did find out: lives are shattered on a daily basis but people forget — and next up was the song "New Girl Now" by Honeymoon Suite. This broke the spell completely. I was now fully myself and I thought: I've always liked what's new. I've never been hypnotised by the spectacle. I've always looked to the future. I've never been held back by nostalgia. I thought: even though I was late for Travel's music lesson, eventually he'll understand. He'll know it was for a better world. That I was taking action for him and his sister. Just like Ganbold said, to free us all from the spectacle. When he's older he'll understand. What would he think of me later if he knew I hadn't at least tried?

SUMMER

10

"Can I get your full name?"

"Florian Moore."

"No middle name?"

"No."

"Is that Moore with an 'e' at the end?"

"Yes."

At this point the door opened and another officer peeked in. "Are you going to be needing me?" he asked.

"No. He's just come in to give a statement," said the first officer. "I just didn't want to be distracted." He was apparently indicating the choice of room — windowless apart from the one-way glass adjacent to the table at which we sat.

The second officer left and it was just me with the first. His head was shaved. He was stocky. His uniform was all black, bulked up — maybe there was a bulletproof vest underneath. Heavy boots, utility belts holding a truncheon on one side and the holster for a pistol on the other. I wondered if he ever used these things. Probably.

He sat in a swivelling armchair. I sat on a folding chair upholstered with synthetic tweed, padded it seemed with a thin layer of soft foam, useless. I might as well have been sitting on the bare metal frame. It was uncomfortable. The room was institutional — grey on grey. "I'm Constable Xenakis, and here's my card if you need to reach me for follow-up," he said, reaching across the table. "So, this group you're a part of... It's called Defiance?"

"Yes."

"So what is it? Some kind of swingers club?"

"No. It's a performance art group."

"So you, like, do theatre, or what?"

"I guess you can call it impromptu theatre, of a sort."

"And then you like, you know, hook up."

"No. That's not really what we're after."

"Tell me what you mean by 'impromptu theatre.'"

"Well, we create public performances that passersby may not see as 'performances.' I guess you might say we do it to make people's day a bit more interesting."

"And you all get naked."

"At the meetings we do. Not at the performances, necessarily."

"I'd be cautious about that, if I were you."

"Well, I suppose we'd only remove our clothes if it's a place we're allowed to. Like a clothing optional beach."

"I'd hope so. But isn't that kind of kinky? I mean, at your meetings. It sounds like there are lots of women in this group. Don't you get turned on?"

"Well, it's non-sexual nudity. We do it to liberate ourselves from clothes, so —"

"Well, let's get to the point. I've also spoken to…" He enunciated slowly each syllable of Solomiya's name. Then again: "Solomiya. Took me a while to get the hang of that one. Apparently the stress is on the second syllable. Thought it sounded Italian at first — like *sole mio*. Unusual name. Anyway, Solomiya Gura. Is she a good friend of yours?"

"I'd say she's an acquaintance."

"How long have you been in this group?"

"Four or five months, I think."

"So you don't know her too well."

"Not too well. But I wanted to come in today in case there's anything I can say that might be helpful —"

"What's her last name?"

"Who?"

"Solomiya."

"Gura."

"Good."

"I'm not being interrogated, am I?"

"No. Not at all."

"Because I came here to help. I'm concerned that someone might be stalking the women in our group, and if there's anything I can say that might help... Well, I don't want anyone to get hurt."

"Of course not. And I want to let you know you're doing the right thing. I'm glad you came in. The more people I talk to in your group the better. The more I know the better I'll be able to identify the suspect. And feel free to tell me whatever you want. Even if something seems trivial to you, it might be helpful to me."

"Okay."

"So I'm going to continue. What can you tell me about Haruko Rusakova? You know her pretty well?"

"Fairly well, I think. But we met each other by chance again recently, and we had had no contact for about fifteen years. I'm really very new to the group."

"I understand you used to be in a band with her, way back when. Rondo X?"

"Yes."

"I heard of you guys. I used to be into music back in my day. The guy who plays bass in Sucky Charger — he used to be in your band."

"That's right."

"I used to be big into those guys. A real big fan. Well, maybe not, like, a crazy big fan — but I saw a couple of their shows. Really high energy, those guys. I mean *really high energy*. That chick jumping all over the place... And the bass player — he could really whack that thing."

"There's no doubt about that."

"And what about Aileen O'Reilly? How well do you know her?"

"I don't know an Aileen O'Reilly."

"Come on! Aileen? You don't know Aileen?"

"I'm sorry. I've never heard of her."

"It was a joke. Get it? Like the song 'Come on Eileen!' Different spelling, though. I thought you were a big music guy."

"Yes, I got it."

"I'm surprised, though, that you haven't heard of Aileen. She had quite a fall, you know. Solomiya and Haruko seemed to know her pretty well, so I'm surprised you don't. And then there's..." Constable Xenakis flipped through a notepad, searching for names. "Erika Kaiser. Zephyr Young. Zephyr... That's a hippy name if I've ever heard one. Zephyr. She came in here, too. First time I've seen anyone wearing a knitted shawl in at least a few decades. Are you all a bunch of hippies? Is that what it's all about?"

"We have all sorts of people in our group."

"And what about hooking up? You figure maybe some guy in your club wasn't getting enough and —"

"Like I said, that's not the point of our group."

"Those two both reported being chased around by some man in a horse mask. Do you believe that?"

I thought for a moment. "I can't imagine they'd have any reason to lie about it. But I thought Zephyr said it was a different kind of animal — a civet, I think."

"That's right. But let's talk about the horse mask. What was it made of?"

"I don't know. No one gave me a description."

"A Przewalski's horse? Am I saying that right? A Clydesdale? What kind of horse?"

"I don't know. I'm not the one who got followed."

"Then who do you think it was? It seems someone knows or is getting tipped off about where these women are going to be. Who would know that stuff?"

"In theory, no one should know who's doing a performance, because the performance instructions are handed out randomly. Although, if someone wrote the instructions, they would know the location and time."

"There's a guy named Lou... I can barely pronounce his name: Drzewiecki. And the other guy, too. Ganbold Mirzoyan. They seem like ringleader types. Do you figure one of these guys might have more information than the rest of you? Do you figure either of them likes running around in a horse mask, or whatever?"

"I doubt it. I don't think they'd know any more than anyone else. I mean, I don't think there's any way for them to know the locations and times of all the performances — we call them 'actions' — with the exceptions of the ones they write. And then we have some safeguards — at least one other person vetting the instructions. We work like a collective. And I've never heard about Ganbold or Lou showing any particular interest in horses."

"How about you?"

"What about me?"

"Do you like running around in a horse mask chasing after women?"

"If I did I wouldn't be here."

"I know. You're a good guy, Florian. I'm just testing. I have to do my due diligence, you know. And I thank you for coming in. I just want to know who you think did it. If you have an idea. Like, have you noticed a pattern? I mean, something each of these women has in common? They don't all seem to look the same way. Although maybe they were a bit… What about the kind of performance they were doing? Maybe that was it."

"I don't know. I don't know what they were doing when they got followed. Or stalked. But we all contribute 'actions.' So they all have their own flavour. And like I said, they're handed out randomly. They're in envelopes, too. So it would be hard to see someone else's 'action.' But I guess you could say they tend to fall into some different categories: natural environments and rituals, or urban environments especially focussed on things — as in things for sale. We like to critique commodity fetishism. But that's just in my very limited experience. I don't know if that helps."

"Commodity fetishism?"

"Well, that comes from Marx. Basically —"

"Never mind. I'll look it up. Let's talk about Aileen O'Reilly. Does she look good with her clothes off?"

"I don't know. I don't think I've ever seen her. You know, there are a lot of people in this group."

"What about Zephyr Young? Is she hot?"

"It depends on your taste. Look, I came here because I wanted to help. Because I was quite worried by what I heard, and thought that if there's anything I know that might help you identify the attacker —"

"For sure. You're doing a good thing, Florian. We really need more people like you who care, right? Now tell me about Ganbold. I hear he has some kind of communist tattoo or something. Is that right? Is the guy a communist?"

"I don't know. And I don't know how that's relevant."

"But you were just telling me about Marx."

"Sure. But that's not necessarily about political communism. Like being in a communist political party, or something. We steer pretty far away from that in our group. Anyway, if there's something I can tell you related to the women in our group being followed, I think I've answered your questions." I paused for a moment. "I'm wondering how much longer you'll need me here. If you have any more questions that might give help you find the stalker."

"Certainly. And you can leave anytime. I'm sure you want to get on with your day. Again, I want to assure you this isn't an interrogation or anything. And yes — I do have a few more questions. About things that might help us narrow it down to who it was — who it is. I'm on your side. Like I said, I just want to know as much as possible so maybe we can stop whoever it is before somebody gets even more badly hurt."

"So, what more can I tell you?"

"Well, that friend of yours — Haruko. She used to be called Ag- — I can't even pronounce the name. Anyway, she used to have a different name. How about you? Did you used to have a different name? Is this a common thing in your group, to change your names? I want to know because it might be important."

"I've always been Florian Moore. I'm not aware of anyone else in our group having changed their name."

"And about your middle name — did you change that?"

"No. I've never had a middle name."

"And I want you to tell me about the day you had your meeting at Bridge Books."

"Well, there's not much to say. I met Haruko there ahead of time. The meeting went ahead just like other meetings, I suppose. Again, I'm fairly new to the group. From what I understand, meetings always start with a restatement of purpose, some discussion of recent 'actions,' then we create some new 'actions.' "

"Have you been back there recently?"

"No."

"What's the most recent book you got there?"

"Oh... It might have been — I think it was *Nazi Literature in the Americas* by Roberto Bolaño. I don't often buy books these days. We have limited space at home, so I usually just check them out at the library.

"But I thought you were a communist. Are you a Nazi? Is that why you got that book?"

"No. That's not really the point of the book — a Nazi readership. We're all quite anti-Nazi in Defiance."

"Because you're all communists."

"I never said that."

"So, this meeting — is that when you all decided to get naked?"

"Well, until then we had been merely 'clothing optional.'"

"How did you feel about seeing Haruko naked for the first time? Were you worried you might get... you know, turned on?"

"It wasn't the first time."

"So are you two, like, having an affair?"

"No. Do you have any more questions? Because I do have to get on with my day. Because, if you don't have any questions that might be relevant —"

"Those Nazis really like playing with fire... the Reichstag and all that. How about you? Do you like playing with fire?"

"What are you talking about?"

"How about fire sprinklers? Maybe you like playing with water."

"I have no particular interest in fire sprinklers."

"That's good."

"What's this all about?"

"Well, you know that early this morning someone went into Bridge Books and started playing with the fire sprinklers. Wrecked almost the entire inventory."

"I didn't know that."

"What kind of propellant do you like to use?"

"What?"

"Just testing. Sarah Engels, one of the owners — she's a part of Defiance. Is there anyone in your group who might have something against her?"

"Not that I'm aware. She seems to be well liked. But again, I'm new. I don't know what kind of politics might be going on behind the scenes."

"And what about Aileen O'Reilly?"

"What about her? Like I said, I don't know her."

"Does she have a nice rack?"

"I don't see the point. I don't know her. Look — I do have other appointments today. Am I free to go?"

"Yes, of course. You've always been free to go..." Xenakis looked me straight in the eyes. It was almost a challenge.

"Thank you, Florian."

I stood up and walked to the door, attempted to open it, but it was locked. I turned toward Constable Xenakis.

"Oh. You need one of these," he said, holding up a key fob. He got up from his chair very slowly — like he was making a show of it — and very slowly came to the door. Another big production. "Thanks again, Florian. You've done a good thing, coming forward. Hopefully we'll catch whoever it is. I'm sure we will. You have my card, so if there's anything else you think I should know, call me." He opened the door.

I exited the main entrance of the police station, which was on a side street that sloped downward to a wider street lined with towers. Some of these retained, on their lower floors, facades of the Edwardian business blocks they replaced. Some were still in the process of being replaced. The sound of a jackhammer echoed from a block or two away. From about six storeys up the new buildings were mostly glass — mirrored glass. Distinct rays of sunlight — more visible owing to the smoke — shined through gaps in the towers, reflecting off mirrored panels down onto the street. It was midmorning and should have been a hot, bright day but for the smoke of forest fires. The nearest, according to news reports, was about thirty-five kilometres away, in a mountain valley. Wherever one went there was a campfire smell. It seemed out of place in an urban environment. It used to seem out of place, but the fires had become an annual occurrence. People wore anti-pollution masks. Parents were advised to keep children indoors at this time of year. I worried about my children — about their lungs. We bought air purifiers for our apartment.

11

The meeting had started with an incantation, as usual, followed by a review of recent actions. One had taken place in the back room of a small art gallery, where there was an installation of scientific glassware placed on shelves affixed at various heights on all four walls. The glass pieces were filled with various amounts of water to produce, when tapped, various notes on the chromatic scale. The vessels were tapped by floating pins that were attracted by a small electromagnet affixed to their outsides. The order in which they were tapped seemed to be random, reported the actor, and she had no idea how they were activated. Her instructions were "to lay on the bench in the middle of the room and be part of the exhibit." It wasn't a particularly risky job, she told us, because the curator — the gallery's only employee — hardly ever gets around. "He's usually out in the alley, smoking pot," she said. Nevertheless, "one needs to look rather pristine to get away with being an exhibit in an art gallery." It shouldn't have been a hard task for her, I thought; she was rather pristine in her youth. For extra authenticity she decided to dress up for the occasion, in "the kind of clothes one might find in the costume room of an amateur theatre." She was a singer by training so had chosen to wait for one particular note to be played, then respond vocally with the semitone higher. During the half hour or so she was in the room, perhaps only three people stepped in, and none seemed to notice anything was amiss, she told us.

Another action — this one performed by a balding man with browline glasses — had been to feign a sudden ankle injury and fall to the ground in front of a car stopped at a crosswalk. He had had to practice the manoeuvre multiple times in order to make it look "authentic," he told us. The purpose of this action was to prompt the driver to leave their car to assist another human being, and "to disarm the automobile as a weapon of isolation." Although the action had had no such effect — the driver had merely driven around the fallen actor, who was helped by another pedestrian — it drew praise from Ganbold, who reminded us of our mission to confront isolation, the "endless production of inauthentic needs," and "reification of the system's mental weaponry."

The last report, however, consumed far more of our attention. It was from the woman with the long, sandy-coloured hair and the knitted shawl, whose name I then learned was Zephyr Young. What her action was I cannot remember, except that while on it she had encountered a man in an animal mask. It was "a very good mask," she told us, "not just some throwaway you'd find at a discount shop." It was hard to identify the animal — perhaps it was a civet, she said — but it was "eerily real" and fully encapsulated the man's head. At first she thought he might have been part of the action. Ganbold appeared angered to hear this — everybody knows that instructions must disclose all participants and their roles, he said. Others concurred that we should all be aware of the rule, and asked — it seemed rhetorically — if anyone had broken this rule. "But that's not what I'm asking," said Zephyr. It had become fully apparent to her that, no, the man in the mask was not a part of the action. She knew this with certainty when, after the prescribed action was over, the man in the civet mask continued to shadow her, following her at a distance, taking the same turns. Someone asked: hadn't she heard about Erika? No, she hadn't. Solomiya told the story. Zephyr asked why she hadn't been warned, why we hadn't brought this up at a meeting. Then she reached the climax of her story, and broke down in tears. He caught up to me, she said. He was a very fast runner, she said. He grabbed me roughly by the arm, shoved me. Then, from his own pocket he produced a wallet — my wallet, she told us — and threw it down beside me. "Here you go! You dropped this!" he said. And between and before and after these phrases, we were told, the man had uttered some guttural sounds that might have been language, but probably were not. And then he ran off.

After listening to this story, I felt strange. It was a frightening account, and I was very moved by Zephyr's emotion. I think we all were. We talked about what to do. Although we have never viewed the police as our allies, someone said, we need to report this. There can be no more solo actions, said someone else. To this we all agreed.

Despite Zephyr's news, the meeting continued according to the agenda. New actions were created and distributed. Then there was time to socialize, and I spent much of this time speaking with Haruko and Solomiya.

"Come to think of it," said Haruko, "I may have had a similar experience after my last action. There was a man in a mask, although I didn't make much of it. These days lots of people wear anti-pollution masks, now that the forests are burning. Most of them are simple — you know, just fabric over the mouth and nose. But they're turning into fashion accessories. Some are quite elaborate. Some cover the entire face. There are even some made to look like characters from animated movies. What do you call these people? I think *otaku* is the term. Anyway, I noticed a guy with such a mask. It was like an old-fashioned military gas mask, embellished with some whiskers and furry bits. He seemed to be taking the same route home as me. He changed busses twice with me. He was always at a distance, and it may just have been coincidence —"

"It's clear that whoever it is — and it's always a man, probably the same man — is specifically targeting the women in our group," said Solomiya. "Hearing Erika's story, Zephyr's story, and now yours, just now... it makes me feel physically ill."

"I'm not happy to hear Zephyr's story at all," said Haruko. "Now I feel afraid. What if that man in the gas mask —"

"It has to be him," said Solomiya. "The same guy."

"Do you really think so?" I asked.

"Absolutely. The question is this: how does he know who and when and where we're going to be?"

"I feel angry," said Haruko. "I hate it when men treat women this way."

"I'm worried for you," I said. "If someone was following you... What if the same thing had happened? The thing that happened to Zephyr."

"Or worse," said Solomiya. "Which is why I agree with those who say we should go to the police. Even if they are a part of the system we oppose —"

"Well, I think we should," said Haruko, abruptly determined. "I'm thinking of a time when a man treated me like garbage. And for anyone who's ever been hurt — for anyone who might get hurt — I think we have to."

Solomiya confirmed her intention to go to the police. "Sadly," she said, "it seems that someone in our group has been using inside information, somehow. And I can't put it all together right now, but someone with more experience might be able to... and we're the ones who know about our group..."

"If there's something I can do to help, I want to help," I said.

"It would be very powerful if you would make a statement, too," said Solomiya. "We need men on our side. The police — they're mostly men. They're likely to empathize with you, if you come forward."

"But what if we cause trouble for our group?" I asked. "Or for myself. I have a job and a family... I mean, if they — I mean the police — start taking exception to what we're doing here."

"You won't cause any trouble," said Solomiya. "We've done nothing wrong. You've done nothing wrong. There's absolutely nothing illegal about our actions as Naked Defiance. I work for an NGO. I've seen lots of civil disobedience, even some risky civil disobedience, and nothing has ever come to criminal charges. And what we do isn't even what you'd call civil disobedience. It's nothing like that."

"And we have a duty to come forward," said Haruko. "If someone got hurt — I mean really hurt. If not coming forward led to something even worse happening. Then it would be our fault. And then we could, in fact, be in trouble."

"That's right," said Solomiya.

And so I was persuaded. Even more I was obliged. As comrades in Naked Defiance we shared a mandate, and therefore everything else... all else followed. My friends were right. Of course they were.

12

" 'In a public place one swoons while the other plays a saxophone; a passerby and a busker. A cliché? Or, is it antidote to the simulation of life and oceanic falsity thus arising? Only the viewer knows, because the notes are random.' These were our instructions," said Haruko.

"Who played the saxophone?" I asked.

"It happened to be Lou. That is, Lou drew the corresponding card. According to the instructions, either of us could have played the saxophone."

"Does Lou know how to play?"

"No. Which is why we both decided he should play. I'm too musical. It would have been even more surprising for a man to swoon in public as a woman played saxophone, but he likes that kind of thing—playing random notes. He used to be in a noise band. Have you ever heard of The Dupobs?"

"No."

"Well, anyway, he enjoys that kind of thing. He likes making noise, and I can say he's good at it. It's all about personality, rather than musicianship."

"And I imagine you'd be quite good at swooning—to a saxophone. It reminds me of that Kate Bush song."

"I am an actress, and a dancer."

"You don't say 'actor.' "

"No. I say 'actress.' "

"And how did it go?"

"Well, I can say it went quite… well. Although I didn't feel like I was acting. I was thinking about Erika and Zephyr, as we heard at the meeting. And now Aileen. Aileen falling down the stairs. Thinking that I, too, might have been stalked by a man in an animal mask. And after talking with the police. After all that I was feeling quite serious, frightened and preoccupied. So, at any other time, performing like that — like some caricature of a woman swooning before a saxophone — it would have been the mere performance of acting. But this time I simply was. I was at one with the cacophony. It was a pure, oceanic experience — not false at all. I was a part of it. Lou was part of it, too. He was very engaged. One could tell. I think he was feeling just as serious as I was — about the things that have happened. In any event, if I am to comment on how things went — I mean, how the audience took it — I can't really say. I mean, I can say how I felt, but we were oblivious to the audience. Although I know there were people around. It must have been quite an uncanny experience to them. To see this performance that was not at all a performance, but the real thing.

"Who is Aileen?" I asked.

"What do you mean?"

"When I was interviewed I was asked over and over about Aileen O'Reilly. But I don't know who she is."

"How can you not? She's at every meeting. Almost every meeting."

"Maybe I just haven't spoken to her. Or maybe I just don't know her name."

"She's the one who always makes a big entrance. It's almost her signature to throw down all her clothes, raise up her arms, and declare, 'I love being naked!' as soon as she enters the room."

"I don't think I've noticed."

"I thought you would have."

"Maybe I just happened to be out of the room whenever it happened. What does she look like?"

"She has red hair and a light complexion."

"She must be Irish."

"She's Chinese."

"With red hair and a name like Aileen O'Reilly?"

"Her hair isn't naturally red. I mean it's red. Primary red. She dyes it that way. Her Chinese name is Ai-ling.

"Did she marry an O'Reilly?"

"No. It was her mother's last name. Before she met Aileen's biological father — who was also Chinese — her mother had been married to an Irishman who had been working in Hong Kong as a pipefitter. The marriage didn't last long — just months. But for whatever reason Aileen's mother decided to keep her married name. Maybe it was too much hassle to do the paperwork to have it changed back. Or maybe she just liked the name. I never asked."

"Do you know her well?"

"I do. Or I did. Not so much now, but we were childhood friends. Or at least playmates."

"From school?"

"From summer vacation. Every summer we'd go up to a place called Yeti Lodge. Have you heard of it?"

"It sounds familiar."

"It's inside a remote fjord. The only way there is by boat or float plane. It was built about a hundred years ago by some eccentric Bavarian. Some guy who, apparently, emigrated with only some spare change in his pocket then became fabulously rich. I always find it hard believing those stories. Anyway, that's where Aileen's mother worked as a cook. After her biological father left them, Aileen's mother had had enough of Hong Kong. She thought her life there was cursed, so she wanted to get out. She was hired by the Yeti Lodge and got a visa. She worked there for about twenty years. So, aside from the off-season, Aileen was raised in the wilderness. We were the same age and we'd always play together when I visited in the summer, and write each other letters the rest of the time, now and again. While we were playing my dad was off fishing. Sometimes hunting, although he kept that hidden from me. It was a hunting and fishing lodge. That was the one thing I never quite understood about my dad. It seemed completely out of keeping with the rest of him."

Visualizing Haruko in the wilderness with her dad, I was reminded of my own experience — not of wilderness, but of rural life and the only time I ever went hunting. During secondary school I had applied for a student exchange to a rural community. This was done through an organization that arranged reciprocal homestays between rural and urban teenagers. My parents thought it was a good idea, and I was self-motivated. I was sixteen, and had been fascinated by the wilderness for some years, ever since I had been caught stealing supplies from my school's music room and had been directed by the principal to see a psychologist. The psychologist, in turn, assigned me some reading: juvenile fiction — some of it not badly written — on the topic of life in the wild. A surrogate for wilderness therapy. Having lived in a city all my life, it inspired me. Largely the only "nature" I had seen was from the pedestrian safety of a crushed gravel trail through a park. I wondered how it would feel to make my own trail through the woods. I had only ever seen wild animals — bears, wolves, ferrets — in zoos. I wanted to see them free in their own environment.

As it turned out I did get to see some wild animals — at close range, even — although not the way I had imagined. The program found a match in a rural area, a boy my age who would stay with my family for a month while I stayed with his. It was indisputably a rural area — not quite the wilderness, but close enough to the mountains that I could see some wilderness. The family had a large house on about a hectare of land on the outskirts of a small town. I imagine my counterpart must have felt cramped in my parents' three-bedroom walk-up, even though it was large for the city. My homestay parents were not farmers. My homestay mother was a dental receptionist in the town, and the father was a heavy machinery mechanic — there was some forestry and mining nearby. They were nice people. They treated me well. Although puzzled by my interest in the surrounding forest and the animals, they answered my questions with patience — and that applied even to my counterpart's younger brother who found nothing particularly interesting about wild animals, and was far more engaged with science fiction television series than the outdoors. During my last weekend they decided to give me what they thought I wanted: an overnight trip to the wilderness — hunting.

What was I to do? I had no interest at all in killing animals, but it was a case of not wanting to look a gift horse in the mouth. I had wanted to spend some time in the woods. Now that it was being offered, I couldn't exactly lay out any conditions. I remember hearing somewhere that certain Buddhist monks, ostensibly vegetarian, will accept offerings of meat — simply because it's bad form not to receive what is offered. What could I have said? And then we were there, in the forest, waiting quietly. And there was a deer, supernaturally beautiful. I had only ever seen deer in photographs, so this one was just as surprising and strange to me as if I had looked up in the sky to find a spacecraft from *Space: 1999*. And there was the deer, on the ground. My homestay father had shot it. We approached and it was labouring in death. I reached out to stroke its head, compassionately. My host told me to step aside. He finished the deer with a knife across the neck.

"It'll feed us for a while," he told me in the truck on our way home. "This is what people have always done. Hunting. It's very… I think the word is 'elemental.'"

13

When he was taken by the police, Ganbold was with Foreste. They were sunbathing nude in his backyard. We were tired of the smoke, she said. We were tired of being indoors with the hum of the air purifiers. We needed some fresh air, even though it wasn't very fresh. It was a hazy day that should have been a sunny day, but at least it wasn't as dark as it often had been, she said. So they went outside wearing nothing but their anti-pollution masks, and lay down on two reclining deck chairs that Ganbold had put out for the purpose, in order "to get some vitamin D."

They had been there "for some time" when they heard a knock on the door — quite a heavy knock. Someone was pounding on the door, she said, maybe with some kind of heavy object. It could be heard all the way to the back yard. It had a heavy, angry rhythm, but Ganbold was unperturbed. I asked if he was going to answer the door, said Foreste, but he said only that he was "not having guests." He was strangely calm, she told us, "almost as if he had been expecting it to happen."

The pounding stopped, and soon two police officers entered the back yard, from around the side of the house. "They were quite bulked up," said Foreste, "like nothing I had seen before. It was like they were dressed for a riot." They ordered Ganbold to go with them, but he just stayed where he was. "For what?" he asked. "You know what," said one of the police officers. Ganbold asked if he was under arrest, but they evaded the question. You can't just walk onto someone's property without a warrant, he said. Yes we can, they said. There are all sorts of reasons to justify entering your property, they said. Ganbold asked for some examples. They cited the order to stay inside but for "necessary travel" when air quality was this poor. They cited public indecency, because he was outside without any clothes. "But this is my back yard, and no one can see!" he objected. It went back and forth like this for a while, according to Foreste.

Next, one of the police punched Ganbold across the temple and pushed him to the ground. The other got involved. They got him pinned, then tied his hands together behind his back — not with handcuffs, but a plastic cable tie.

"I was screaming at them at this point," said Foreste. "They dragged him to the front of the house, where the car was. It was a truck, actually, or an SUV. I could see blood. There was blood on his face. They told me to shut up and go inside. Some neighbours had come out. Ganbold was naked. He was bleeding. They shoved him into the car. I was naked. I was yelling, uselessly. People were watching. They were way harder on him than they needed to be."

Foreste had contacted me by telephone to recount her story, and she had told Haruko, too. She didn't know who else to talk to, she said. We had gotten closer to Foreste at recent meetings — close enough to exchange phone numbers, although I had almost everyone's number at that point. We were all supposed to be friends, to be able to contact one another — especially since Zephyr reported her meeting with the man in the civet mask — so that we could call for help, in case an action went awry.

Foreste told me she would attempt to visit Ganbold at the police station, where she imagined they must be keeping him. I didn't tell Foreste I had been there just the previous week — but

I asked whether Solomiya had heard the news. Foreste said she didn't know, that she hadn't contacted Solomiya. "I don't always feel comfortable talking to her," she said.

———————

As it turned out, Solomiya had not heard the news. "But I'm not surprised," she said.

"What do you mean?" I asked.

"Well, as I told you before, there's always been a kind of unwholesomeness about Ganbold."

"I'm not sure if I've ever seen that."

"You haven't been around long enough."

"But do you really think he would —"

"Look. The police don't just show up and take you away for no reason. They're under a lot of public scrutiny these days. They're not going to mess up. They'll have solid reasons. Just like when you see a patrol car with its lights flashing — you know they're not just wanting to get to the doughnut shop by a certain time. They have their reasons. If a firetruck is racing down the street with its sirens blaring, there's a fire somewhere. If an ambulance shows up and the paramedics take you away, then you know you must be sick. It all follows. They have their reasons, and I'm sure they did their due diligence with Ganbold."

"But Foreste told me she had had a similar experience — being stalked by some guy in an animal mask. I mean, if that's what it's all about."

"What kind of a mask was it?"

"A red slender loris. I think that's what she said."

"That's far too specific."

"But do you really think he would stalk his own girlfriend?"

"No. And I don't think she was stalked. I think she's covering for him. For sure. She's worried that he's the stalker, and that the police have figured it out."

"But according to Foreste they wouldn't say what it was all about — why they were taking him away. I wonder if there might not be some other reason?"

"I think you're in denial."

I considered for a moment, then responded: "You know, I really like Ganbold."

"It's hard, Florian. I know." Suddenly there was a tone of compassion in her voice. "Someone you respected. And then you find out —"

"You're very certain."

"Trust me, Florian. I know. I feel quite strongly about this. Sometimes one just knows. You know? I have my experience, and I know. You have your experience — things you just know. So you have to believe people when they're speaking from their experience. When someone feels so strongly about something, it's probably true. No — it's true. It's true. And now that Ganbold is away, you'll see. There won't be any more animal masks. No more falling down stairs. They took him away for a reason. There won't be any more stalking. You'll see. Absolutely. It's going to stop."

14

It was a confusing time. Or perhaps it was simply a time when I felt caught up in the intensity of what those around me were feeling — those in Naked Defiance. I felt distracted. I remember filling an ice cube tray with water and putting it in the microwave oven, returning an hour later expecting it to be frozen, checking the freezer but not finding it there, then realizing my mistake. That's a memory I have, but it might have been a dream. Or simply a metaphor — regardless of whether it occurred during my waking or sleeping life. In any event, it would be impossible now to verify in which compartment of my life this ice cube event happened. The point being — or maybe it's not the point — that dreams and reality (or so-called reality?) seem to blur together in my recollections of this time in my life.

I was also fined for not wearing a bicycle helmet. Or I had a dream about being fined for not wearing a bicycle helmet. I should be able to verify which quite easily by reviewing my bank account transactions from the time. Certainly I would have had to mail in a cheque. Whichever the case — dream or "reality" — is immaterial. (Even though there may be some *material* for verification.) The fact is my feeling; my very strong recollection of the event.

I was riding my bicycle. It should have been a very short trip — to the pharmacy, just three blocks away. (Our daughter, Trudi, had a mild fever.) I figured I could get away with not wearing a helmet over such a short distance, and normally the police turn a blind eye to cyclists not wearing helmets — but not this time.

Roughly halfway to my destination another rider pulled up beside me. "Florian, is that you?" he said. I looked over and saw that it was Constable Xenakis.

"I didn't know you patrolled by bicycle," I said.

"I do, sometimes. Why don't you stop right up here, on the sidewalk."

I complied. We both came to a stop on the sidewalk, straddled our bicycles. Xenakis did a U-turn in order to face me.

"Is this some kind of 'action' of yours?" he asked.

"What?"

"Not wearing a helmet. Is this some kind of protest against the helmet commodity? Against the helmet as reified state control over the cyclist?"

"Not intentionally."

"One would have to ask why you chose that particular target — the helmet. Wouldn't it have been more original to go cycling without a *bicycle*? Or even just without *clothes*? But I suppose it's a good thing you didn't. Didn't ride without clothes, I mean. We have some pretty strict laws against public indecency. For not wearing a helmet it's merely a fine. I've been wondering why you guys go after some commodities but not others. Aren't they all interchangeable? Or maybe it's risk-aversion that guides you."

I decided not to answer. In such cases — with such people — it's better not to say anything, if one can help it.

"Anyway, I've been reading up about this 'commodity fetishism' you mentioned. Interesting stuff. Seems it's all tied up in semiotics: signifiers, signifieds. Symbols. Commies and Nazis are big into that stuff. Hammers and sickles, swastikas."

"We're neither communists, nor Nazis."

"I didn't say you were. I'm just talking about those things — those people. Commies and Nazis. They're kind of like their own walking symbols. They have their own paraphernalia, and then you know what they're all about. One neat and easy package. I was reading this novel about cults, by Houellebecq —"

"No! Not Houellebecq!"

"You got something against him?"

"Of course I do. He's too right-wing."

"Only if you're standing upside down. Anyway, cults. They've got their signifiers and their signifieds. Which brings me back to the commodity fetish, to the 'misty realm of religion,' which is I think how Marx put it. Crosses, hammers, sickles, swastikas, 1965 Ford Mustangs. Hard, fixed, non-malleable. So let me say I understand your attraction to the idea. Your critique of it. Your group still has some critical distance — for now. Like you say, you're not a bunch of commies. Or Nazis. I've met a lot of your group. I've checked them all out. Soft, round, flexible, malleable... Let me say, I'd sure like to get my hands on some of those commodities — if you know what I mean. Although I might not go so far as putting on a horse mask or something."

He has a one-track mind, I thought.

"Anyway, here's a ticket. A living signifier — of a fine. That's a real thing: money."

"Is it?"

"Well, not really. They say that if everyone went to the bank and tried to withdraw all their cash at the same time, only about five percent would succeed — there's even less real money in the world than there were lifeboats on the Titanic. But you still have to pay. Or you might spend some time in the slammer. And that's a real, concrete thing. Get it? Signified. Or perhaps I should say, 'identified.' Identifiers and identifieds, as seems to be the trendy lingo these days. I notice a lot of your group are really into that shit. Starting to see themselves as reifications of eternal martyrdom. Starting to get a bit inflexible about the idea. Maybe they're turning into their own commodities. I'd be careful if I were you. You might not, but I can tell a lot of your group — regardless of what they say — seem alienated from their spirit essences, or whatever. Despite their hippy haircuts, it's not all peace and love. I'm sure they don't see humanity as one oceanic whole. But I'm sure you know just as much as I do — if not more. Right?

Around the same time as I got fined for not wearing a bicycle helmet, I took part in another Naked Defiance action. Or I dreamed the action. It's hard to say. These actions were all ephemeral — they left no physical evidence. Not at their locations, anyway. Perhaps if a costume was involved, one might have taken it away as a memento, as proof the event happened. But not this action.

I was to meet someone at a train station — I had no idea who it would be. We were to find one another. The other would be wearing a red hat. But not me. (I would have no memento.) The other would find me with their eyes. They would know I was the one because I would be watching them from the other side of a waiting lounge. We would walk toward each other slowly, "mindfully," gazing at each other "like teenagers in mad love." We would hold out our hands to one another, stand face to face holding hands. I had no script. I was simply to repeat exactly what the other told me, slowly, phrase by phrase:

Again. In this life. In this real life. Reality comes closer. Reality arrives. A strange feeling. It must be strange. It was meant to be.

My interlocutor was Haruko. She asked, "Do you think it's a coincidence we've been in all these actions together? Or did someone plan it this way?"

Author's Second Note to Publisher

In a second note to "Mr. Agarwal," the author indicates he hadn't yet heard back about the first. He writes he has "had some thoughts about the clarity of the story" and that a second passage, likewise addressed to the reader, might be inserted between chapters 14 and 15. He expresses his willingness "to make other appropriate modifications as deemed necessary." The second passage follows. – PS

Jorge Luis Borges said this:

I think one should work into a story the idea of not being sure of all things, because that's the way reality is. If you state a given fact and then say that you know nothing whatever of some second element, that makes the first fact a real one, because it gives the whole a wider existence.

Fair enough. But I'm reading through this manuscript (again), and I think perhaps too much is missing, too much is unknown. So far I've been scrupulous to present only my limited perspective — that is, my point of view during the timeframe in which the story took place — aside from some flashbacks, aside from my reports of what others have said, which may have been embellished. Now, however, very soon — here — I'm going to add, in contravention of what Borges prescribed for storytelling, a "second element." Audiences — most audiences, I think — don't agree with Borges, anyway. They want to know everything in order to regard the story as "real." They demand a certain reality. A photorealistic reality, down to every wrinkle — every wrinkle of the author's foreskin, even. Right down to the evolutionary biology of those microscopic living organisms that live on human skin. Following this line of argument, one day the author will need to lie on an exam table… Well, something like that is going to happen in this book, if you read it right through.

So I want to tell more, to bring this story to a more precise "reality" — and not only that. I also want to bring it to a higher word count, to make it sellable in an age of standardization — 40,000 words, at least, is the standard for a novel. And for a novel that pretends to say something about commodities, it makes sense to match the commodity standards of our age. Most importantly, of course, I want to make this book easier to read.

Prior to the invention of standardized shipping containers, longshoremen — longshore*people*, or longshore*workers* — used to have to figure out how everything would fit. On a similar topic, in real life I once took an aptitude test to be hired as a clerk for a major grocery store chain. The test was to fit a number of differently-sized items into a box in a certain amount of time, and I failed.

I don't want you to fail at reading this book.

And now for the "second element," which is Solomiya's story: I'm going to make it clearer, because I don't want to leave it a mystery. When I wrote the first draft, I thought you might want to guess what was happening behind the scenes. Now, however, I think you might want to know with certainty how Solomiya mobilized a faction within Naked Defiance.

As fear intensified regarding the animal masks, Solomiya organized a "Naked Defiance women's discussion group." I knew about it because Haruko went to the preliminary meeting, "to bear witness," as she said. As far as I know, that was the only meeting she attended. She said it was clear Solomiya held all the cards, so to speak; that Solomiya was the "charismatic leader" and there wasn't much if any room to influence the group's direction.

To clarify, during the timeframe of this story I knew nothing of the group's activities beyond their initial meeting, and it wasn't until long after that I learned the true extent. It seems that after assessing the loyalties of those who had attended the "discussion group," a core group was formed. Consisting of current or former members of Naked Defiance, this covert splinter group tested out the names "Real Commodities" and "Womyn's Research Collective" before settling on "Womyn's Defiance Brigade" (WDB). Its five members were Solomiya, Erika (Erika Kaiser of the supermarket incident recounted in Chapter 8), two other women whose names were not revealed to me, and also a man named Brnóþ Green, who I may or may not have met before. Any details I learned came through Erika, who I met in another chance supermarket encounter following the timeframe of this story.

By Erika's account, the group worked, at the outset, to develop an ideological framework with an emphasis on "womyn's decommodification." For a time they focussed on developing actions within this ideological framework, but parallel to the "generalist output" of Naked Defiance. Soon, however, according to Erika, Solomiya "asserted her dominance" and the group started moving in a "strangely ambiguous" direction, in which "the line between irony and sincerity was blurred." One action was to attend a rally in support of women's right to wear face coverings in public: "Even as an insider," said Erika, "I was unsure what we were really trying to say on this topic." Such actions, said Erika, reminded her somehow of the Futurists: "Frightening, clever, funny... hard to know which. But clearly frightening, after a time."

Indeed, things started taking a dark turn when Brnóþ started showing "almost hysterical adherence," in Erika's words, to

Solomiya's increasing emphasis on "balancing oppression." At one meeting Brnóþ sealed his mouth shut with duct tape, because, as he explained prior to the performance, "The world has heard enough — too much, in fact — from men." And then, said Erika, some of these performances became even more extreme. One time he declared he wanted to be "a sacrifice, like Jesus Christ," and Solomiya chastised him violently in front of the whole group, for daring to equate what they were doing with religion. "The whole thing was creepy," said Erika. "I still find it hard to talk about. There was more. Even worse. But I don't even want to talk about it."

It was also clear, said Erika, that Solomiya had "other motives." Whenever Solomiya raised the topic of "oppression," she inevitably steered the conversation toward Ganbold. "I never got along too well with Ganbold," said Erika. "But I also don't think he was as bad as Solomiya made out." When it came to Ganbold, said Erika, "At least I always felt that our differences were collegial. After a time, I don't think I could say the same for my differences with Solomiya. And I'm not into take-downs, which is what I think she was after. So I stopped going to meetings, and Solomiya never called me back."

15

"I don't think he did it. I just spoke to Lou." It was Haruko again — this time *not* in a dream. I am certain of it. She was on the telephone.

"You mean the animal masks? I don't think anyone suspects Lou," I said.

"No. I mean Ganbold. I don't think Ganbold did it. Lou just got stalked. It happened this morning. And Ganbold was already in jail, or wherever they're keeping him."

"What happened to Lou? The same pattern?"

"Exactly. A guy in a civet mask. Lou got really spooked. He said it looked quite realistic. It scared him, it looked so real. He said it really was like the head of a civet on a man's body. Its mouth opened and closed, it had saliva and a tongue and everything. It had real fur."

"But that guy's always on mushrooms," I said.

"The guy in the civet mask?"

"No. Lou. Maybe he hallucinated it."

"Have you ever been on mushrooms?"

"Well, back in my band days I did a lot of things. But no — I've never taken mushrooms."

"That's just some stereotype people have. 'Hallucinogen' is probably a misnomer. It's not like you're going to see something that's physically not there. It's more of a feeling. Of connectedness. If anything, things become more real. Although I have seen tyres breathing…"

"So, is he all right? What happened?"

"Like I said, the same pattern. The guy in the animal mask can be seen at a distance. Then you notice that he's taking the same route you are. Then you try to avoid him but he's still there. The same thing happened to Lou."

"Was he hurt?"

"No. And he probably didn't need to worry, I'm sure."

"He's a big guy."

"Yeah. Almost two metres. And not exactly skinny. But even still, he was scared."

"I understand. I would have been scared, too. Sometimes even very small animals can frighten you. I get frightened even by woodlice, never mind a man with the head of a civet. How did he get away?"

"They ended up somehow at the Bridge Building. Lou ran inside, hoping to find a shop open and ask for a place to hide. But all the doors were locked. It was early in the morning. Almost all those places wait until eleven o'clock to open up. The only door that was unlocked was at that workshop Zephyr runs."

"What workshop is that?"

"You know the place with all the sewing machines, light tables, woodworking tools and such? Where you can use all the stuff for a donation?"

"Zephyr runs that place?"

"You didn't know?"

"No."

"Anyway, she usually leaves it unlocked. She's really trusting. She wants to make sure anyone can use it, whenever they need. So Lou went in there, and he's feeling very guilty about it."

"Why?"

"Well, if Zephyr had been there —"

"Then the guy in the civet mask would see her and he'd know where she worked."

"Exactly. But fortunately she wasn't there, and Lou was able to hide in a closet."

"Did the guy come in?"

"Apparently, but he didn't look around for long."

"It's a good thing. With all those tools in there…"

"So, what I'm saying, Florian, is that it couldn't have been Ganbold."

"No. I suppose it couldn't. And Foreste had a similar experience, and why would he stalk her? That doesn't make sense, either."

"It doesn't make sense, and I'm very worried for Ganbold. And I think we did the wrong thing."

"What?"

"Going to the police."

"Yes, I see. I was thinking the same."

"They won't even tell Foreste where he is. They say they'll release information only to 'next of kin.' So she's tried to get help from some civil liberties association, but they hardly seem interested."

"Does he have any 'next of kin' around here?"

"All I know is that he has a sister. I'm going to do some asking around. I have no idea who she is, where she is, whether she's been informed… I'm really worried for Ganbold. Once the police have you in there, they could do anything and nobody would know."

"That's not how Solomiya sees things. She says there's lots of oversight, and she's pretty convinced Ganbold is the one."

"That's what I was going to say next. We need to talk some sense into her. That Xenakis creep isn't going to listen to you or me, but he might listen to her."

"You felt that way about him, too."

"Isn't it obvious? But Solomiya couldn't see through him, somehow. She comes off as pretty astute the first few times you meet her. Now I'm really starting to wonder."

"But she seems quite certain that she's right. Do you really think we're going to change her mind?"

Haruko said we were "going to have to try" and that she wanted me to be with her when she approached Solomiya. Solomiya was the key, she said. Solomiya had a "connection" with Xenakis, and a lot of influence in our group. If we could just get her to go back to Xenakis, maybe he'd be reasonable. But if he wouldn't help us, and if the civil liberties association wouldn't help us, then we'd need a lot of us making a fuss. That Ganbold could get hurt if we didn't help him soon. "If he gets hurt," she said, "we'll be responsible in some way."

16

"Lou was stalked?" It was Solomiya speaking. She had agreed to meet us at Zephyr's workshop. It was generally unused at certain times of the day, so it would be private. We sat across from one another at a light table, adjacent to a table saw, among the sewing machines. "Lou's a man," she continued.

"What does that have to do with it?" asked Haruko.

"He's not a woman."

"So?"

"Ganbold — or whoever it is — has only ever stalked women."

"That's not to say he wouldn't start stalking men."

"Lou's always on mushrooms. Maybe he hallucinated it."

"He's actually quite rational, even when he's on mushrooms. Probably more rational."

"What kind of animal mask was the guy wearing?"

"Civet."

"How would Lou know a civet from any other animal?"

"He's studying for a PhD in Zoology. He knows a lot about animals."

"What's his specialty?"

"Neuroendocrinology. He spends a lot of time chopping off frogs' heads."

"That doesn't mean he knows what a civet's head looks like. And, anyway… It's not very original, is it? Every time it's been a different animal. A horse, some kind of *anime* gas mask thing, a loris. Zephyr got stalked by a civet. It's never been the same animal twice."

Here I interjected, or maybe I *interloped*: "Based on Zephyr's description, it was an Asian civet."

"With Lou it was an oriental civet," Haruko continued.

Solomiya: "What's the difference?"

"There's a big difference."

"I find it hard to believe."

"That the Asian and the oriental civet are so different?"

"No! That Lou would have been stalked by a guy in a civet mask."

"And Foreste had the same thing happen, so —"

"Foreste! What kind of animal was it with her?"

"I forget."

"Look. Doesn't it seem clear to you that Lou and Foreste are just trying to cover for Ganbold?"

"But what about the other questions?" said Haruko. "Would Ganbold have stalked his own girlfriend? And how could he have stalked Lou, if he's in jail? What if he's not the one? Shouldn't we try to help him, if there's any doubt?"

(At this point I considered, momentarily, whether there might in fact be a creature with a civet's head and a man's body. Perhaps that could explain...)

Solomiya continued: "Little Marie Antoinette is sad that she can't be with her boyfriend. She's in denial that he's done something wrong. Doesn't want to go back to —"

"Marie Antoinette? What do you mean by that?" asked Haruko.

"Haven't you heard? For someone who claims to be so repelled by the spectacle — well, you should see the spectacular clothes he buys her! I think the latest was a silk *kimono* he had sent all the way from Japan. A very nice one."

"Well, don't you think a woman... a woman in love has a right..." Haruko bent her head. Her elbows were resting on the table. She pressed her fingers to her temples, then raised her head again. "Anyway, clothing and gifts have nothing to do with this. Our concern here is Ganbold — that he's in police custody, he's in danger, and he's probably not the one... What I care about is making sure we get the right one, before someone gets even more seriously hurt."

"What I care about is sending a message. That I'm here for the victims. And I don't think there is any doubt," said Solomiya. "Constable Xenakis has been very thorough, and he wouldn't have taken him in if he didn't think there was a clear safety risk to the women in our group. He cares a lot for our welfare, you know."

"That's not the impression I got."

"Well, that's the impression I got. He cares a lot about women. He knows a lot about women. He was birthed by a woman, and he told me half the people in his family were women. His sister, his mother, two grandmothers, four great grandmothers... He feels a lot of empathy for women and he doesn't like to see us victimized. Doesn't like to see us oppressed."

"That's how they're trained to talk, in interrogations," said Haruko. "Even though it wasn't officially an interrogation. They're supposed to make you feel like they see the world the same way you do, to get you to loosen up."

Here I offered: "He tried to do that to me, too. He tried to talk to me the way he thought I saw the world, but it backfired. He might have talked to you like he cared about women. But he talked to me pretending to be one of my 'buddies,' like I joined Defiance just so I could see some tits."

"Didn't you?" asked Solomiya. "And don't call them 'tits.' That's really disrespectful to women's bodies."

"I was just using the voice he used," I explained.

"That's the way a misogynist talks."

"I'm not a misogynist."

"Are you sure? You don't seem to be aware of a lot of things, Florian. But maybe I shouldn't be surprised. When I was at the Battle of Seattle, what were you doing? Selling imported health food cereals?"

"What's wrong with that?" I asked.

"Solomiya," said Haruko. "I think we're getting off-topic. Again."

"Sure we are. So, let's get back on topic. And the topic is this: Haruko and Florian, I think you're really in denial. I know you want me to doubt that Ganbold's the one who has been stalking our women. I don't know how you can doubt… when it's so obvious. So obvious. Who else would wear an animal mask and… ? You've even seen him wearing an animal mask! Unless you don't remember.

"When?" asked Haruko.

"That time — you know, when we were in the 'idiolalia parade,' which is what I think he called it. When we walked the downtown all in a line, with paper bags over our heads, yelling non-words in sequence, grunting…"

(Recalling this action brought back a pleasant memory for me, of a strangely oceanic bonding…)

"Well," Solomiya continued, "there was one of us not wearing a paper bag, but rather an animal mask. A wild boar mask. Ganbold was wearing a boar mask. Don't you remember?"

"No. I don't remember. I don't remember it that way at all. How can you know? Were you even anywhere near him in the line?"

"I know because I know. I'm sure, and I'm sure because I was there. Because I was looking. Weren't you looking? Or maybe you didn't want to see. Maybe you don't want to remember."

"Memory is open to question, Solomiya. And yours is certainly different from mine."

"Well, I don't care what you think, Haruko. About your opinion — which is all it is. That's my memory of the event, and it's a true memory. It's your memory that's clouded — by wanting to defend Ganbold, to present some doubt. And I know you want me to talk to Constable Xenakis, and try to convince him, too, that there might be some doubt — that Ganbold should be free until we know for sure who's been stalking our women. But I won't. I know what I know. I remember what I remember. I know what I remember. I remember what I know. I know what I feel. I feel it. I really feel it — that Ganbold is the one. And there's more. There's a lot I know that you don't. We didn't know Ganbold, but we knew his family. Back in Cyprus. A bakery in Limassol —"

" 'We?' "

"My people. My family."

"I didn't know you were from Cyprus. Are you Greek?" asked Haruko.

"No."

Here I re-entered the conversation: "Are you Turkish?" (I thought it might be possible.)

"No! Neither. We weren't from there, originally. That has nothing to do with anything, anyway. But I'll tell you what does have something to do with something: people like him. You don't know what they're capable of. They can be very devious if they don't get their way. They'll keep pushing, and pushing. They'll burn down whole cities."

"What are you talking about?" asked Haruko.

"I'm talking about the Siege of Kiev. Not the Battle of Kiev. The Siege of Kiev. They bombarded the city with catapults, breached the walls. People ran for their lives, took shelter in the Church of Tithes. It collapsed under their weight. The invaders razed almost everything, slaughtered almost everyone."

"Wasn't that almost eight hundred years ago?"

"Sure it was. But perhaps you know that in Kraków, every hour on the hour, from the tallest tower of St. Mary's Basilica, they play a trumpet call, interrupted halfway through the melody. Why? Because the original trumpeter, in 1241, was shot in the throat by an arrow while playing the same melody. He was trying to warn of the approaching Mongolian army when he was cut off. So they haven't forgotten in Kraków, and we haven't forgotten either. And I can tell you the descendants of Subutai haven't changed much since then. I can tell you also that I'm no fan of Stalin, but he was right to push them out of Crimea, finally. And I don't need you to try to convince me otherwise about Ganbold. I know I'm right. I know I'm right, and you can be sure I'm not going to help you get him out of trouble. This is my movie now."

"What do you mean by that?" asked Haruko.

"What I mean by that," Solomiya continued, "is that you've been seeing things your way, your perspective. Your people have been reading this story from your perspective, but there's another layer. Another reality. And in that reality — this reality — I'm the main protagonist. The sympathetic one. And this is the story — it's the actual story that's going to happen — I'm the one who gets my way and all my friends — all of society, even — make a circle around me and they applaud me for what I've achieved, and especially for all the obstacles I've had to overcome in order to get my way. Like him — Florian — battling for your mind. He might look like he's just come along for the ride, but in the end he's just like every other man. And what do you think of men, Haruko?"

"Well, if you don't mind me saying so, I like men. And they don't seem to have a problem with me, either."

(At this point I couldn't help being reminded of a song by the band Missing Persons, mingled with ineffable regret for being seen as a disposable interloper.)

"Whether I mind is beside the point. The point is that you think a lot of things, Haruko. But thinking is not the same as knowing. You'll see. But that's your story, and this is mine: all the things holding me back, extending the route to my story's conclusion. Men — Ganbold, Florian, whoever — are a source of conflicted loyalties."

(Certainly she had overplayed my agency.)

"You think Ganbold is innocent," she continued. "You think Florian is different from the other men. You watch. You'll see. But prior to that point you'll talk against me, attempt to reduce my influence. Perhaps one of your over-zealous followers will lock me in a room somewhere. A room full of animal masks. Have you ever thought about what all those masks represent? Animals. Animals that will soon be extinct. And who's to blame for that? Men. Animals are going extinct due to the actions of men. And Ganbold — yes, I do think the stalker is Ganbold — makes a mockery of these blameless creatures. Anyway, back to the story — the room with the animal masks. When you realize the truth you'll scramble to find the room. You'll discover where I'm trapped. Then you'll see for yourself the incriminating evidence, and you'll know I was right. You'll see me out. But even before that, the building will be on fire. You'll run inside regardless, to find the room. Maybe it's the Bridge Building. Someone — a man — will attempt to drag you out, tell you it's crazy to run into a building on fire. It might be Florian. Maybe he'll be the one who's set the building on fire. You'll kick him between the legs — really hard, I hope — temporarily disarming him, and you'll run on to find me, find the room in which I'm trapped. The room full of animal masks. And you'll hammer down the door with an axe, save me just in time. Just in time to leave for Ganbold's trial, to take me to Ganbold's trial, where I'll hand over the incriminating evidence — a bag full of masks. There might be a traffic jam, or a flat tire. So I'll get out of the car and run. But I'll get there in time. And then I'll win. Then I'll get my round of applause. Then you'll know this is my movie. Which is what I mean by this being my movie. It's my movie. It's my movie now, and I don't need to say any more because I know I'm right. Because I'm right, and you're wrong, eventually you'll see you're wrong, and now I'm the one whose people are looking in on this story, which is all about me."

Solomiya left the room, and Haruko and I sat quietly for a number of minutes.

"Do you think she's right?" I asked.

"Of course not," said Haruko. "She's gone completely mental. Completely beyond rational argument. It's as if…" Haruko said the next two sentences as if to herself: "She's become the signifier for a fixed position. Or a fixed signifier for a position."

"I didn't know Ganbold was Mongolian," I said. "He doesn't look Mongolian."

17

Altantsetseg "Alta" Vynnychenko, née Mirzoyan, worked for the local branch of a major international bank as a "Personal Wealth Adviser." This was the title indicated on her business card. Haruko showed it to me. She had visited the branch in question, taken the card from a display case. I pondered aloud whether we shouldn't just make an appointment — even though I had no plausible reason to visit a wealth consultant. Haruko suggested that Ganbold's sister was probably just a glorified teller, the barrier to meet her would be low, but the real deterrent was time: Alta wasn't booking appointments until next week, and we needed to talk to her right away. It was the weekend and it would look suspicious to wait outside the bank until closing, so we resolved to visit her at home, which was surprisingly easy to find. There was only one Vynnychenko in the phone book — an S. Vynnychenko, which matched up with a Sergiy "Serge" Vynnychenko indicated as "Chief Marketing Officer" at the regional headquarters of the same bank. The address in the phonebook indicated a house in a posh neighbourhood. It was surprising they hadn't opted out of a phonebook listing.

"That's a name someone might have in Kiev," said Haruko. "I've been reading up on that history. The Khans, from what I understand, were always willing to adapt to local customs."

(Here I felt that perhaps I, too, should have done some reading on the subject...)

The house was in an old neighbourhood, on a street lined and shaded by tall trees—oak, chestnut, maple. The lots in the area were generally large—up to half a hectare, I estimated. Many had succumbed to "infill housing," but the Vynnychenko house was among the holdouts. It had been built in a style referred to locally as "neoclassical." It was symmetrical and imposing, a large two storeys set upon a high foundation, with a high-pitched roof. Perhaps it was more storeys. It had multipaned windows with dark grey frames. The façade was largely white, and the entrance had round pillars.

The house was roughly in the middle of its lot, its backdrop more trees like those lining the street. Access was by a wide, cobbled driveway. It was a circular driveway lined with rhodo-dendrons, then in bloom. It circled a fountain, dry, its bottom scattered with rhododendron petals, white and pink. The forests were still burning. It hadn't rained for about three weeks. The city had banned "non-essential" water use. The plants here were still green, but were showing the strain. The smoke in recent weeks had lightened, but it was still hazy. I was seeing the Vynnychenko house as through a soft focus lens.

"I have never understood why it's so easy for some people to have so much money," said Haruko.

"Neither have I. But they have good taste." I was referring to their cars.

———————

Beside the house was a detached garage, with room for two cars. The door was up, and one car had been rolled out. It was a 1973 Citroën SM, colour code AC 637 Bleu de Brégançon Métallisé. I knew all about this car. Someone was waxing it. He was in white coveralls, and it seemed he had arrived in a small van (a Ford Transit Connect, if I remember correctly) with the name of a "mobile auto detailing" business stenciled on its side. As we walked up the driveway he greeted us in a friendly way, as if we were familiar guests. (If only he knew, I thought.) He seemed comfortable there, working on the Citroën, as if he were a regular. The car was pristine. It was a strange and beautiful car — it always would be. It had hydropneumatic suspension with adjustable ride height. It was in the high position, perhaps so it could be polished more easily, so the worker wouldn't have to bend so much. Its headlights, beneath their aerodynamic covers, swivelled with the steering. It had a very sleek dashboard — one that could hardly look dated. I had seen the dashboard in pictures. I had always wanted to sit inside a Citroën SM. Its credited designer, Robert Opron, is said to have been well-liked by his colleagues, to have married well, to have lived a charmed life...

Still in the garage was the other car — a 1975 NSU Ro 80, orange. It was apparently the last European car to be produced with a rotary engine. Felix Wankel had a hand in the engine's design. He was fond of the Nazi party and had been allowed to join the SS for a time. I wondered if these things mattered in the context of car design. Did it matter to Vynnychenko? The Ro 80's overall designer, Claus Luthe, had stabbed his own son...

Now we met Sergiy Vynnychenko, chief marketing officer, and he looked just like I imagined someone would look — someone high up in a bank.

"No. She can't come to the door," he said. His tone was abrupt, almost angry.

We said something about wanting to talk to his wife about her brother.

"You're too late," he said. "He's dead. They killed him. The police killed him."

"We wanted to help —" I said, stupidly.

"Are you going to bring him back to life? No. He's dead. Do you know what that means?" He paused, stared us down, then continued: "I know who you are. I don't care that you 'wanted to help.' I know what your group did. And now he's dead. Ganbold is dead. They put him away, and then they killed him. So, what can you do now? He was my wife's only living relation. What can you possibly say to her now? She wants to be left alone. I want to be left alone. We want nothing to do with you now. That means go. Go. Go, and don't visit us again."

18

We walked away from the house. Our pace, from
what I can remember, was somewhat brisk — although not as fast
as if we were late for an appointment. It was brisk, but aimless.
We had been commanded to leave the Vynnychenko house,
and we had achieved that. We seemed to be walking vaguely
in the direction of the nearest train station — the one at which
we had met perhaps an hour prior. Now we were walking, and
neither of us spoke. We may have exchanged platitudes. I might
have said "I can't believe it," or some other nonsense. Clearly
there was nothing that needed to be said.

At the edge of the posh neighbourhood was a moderately sized
rectangular park. It was a very long and thin rectangle — more
like a line. It was a boundary, really. On the other side was
another kind of neighbourhood with apartment buildings, a
train station, parking lots, abandoned shopping carts, and a
proliferation of bars. Construction cranes and revving engines.
Earlier, on our way from the station, we had passed by a rental
apartment where some carpenters were unloading their tools.
A tenant, on his way out, remarked to them: "That'll do about
as much good as taking a corpse to a dental appointment."
Indeed, the building looked very run down, as did the entire
neighbourhood. But we weren't there yet.

At one end of the park — at one end of the buffer zone — was a
small Japanese garden. I can't say how authentic it was. A plaque
announced that some fifty years prior the director (curiously
unnamed) of the city's Parks Department had been quite fond
of Japanese gardens, so established one on the site. It had a few

large cedar trees, some cherry and plum. Their petals had long since fallen, turned brown, and accumulated in corners. The park appeared to be maintained, but not exactingly. There were ferns and moss, but they seemed to be drying out. (Again, it had been very dry and the surrounding forests were still burning, and there was smoke in the air.) There was a central mound with a labyrinth-like hedge, but it was in need of trimming. We walked up it, then down, but with no feeling. There was a pond. Two carp rested side by side at its bottom, motionless.

"How do we know they are still alive?" I asked.

"If they weren't alive," said Haruko, "I believe they would be floating."

This was, I think, our only spoken exchange while at the garden.

On the other side of the park, running its length, was a major road. Its din had filled the Japanese garden. Now we were walking toward it, through a parking lot adjacent to the garden. The parking lot was the extension of a street that intersected the road — so there was a four-way intersection with a pedestrian-controlled crosswalk. We were walking out of the parking lot, on the left side of the street, and I was walking on Haruko's left side. I pressed the button for the walk signal, it came on, and we started to cross the road.

No cars had stopped on the road to our left — there had been a gap in traffic — and I was walking on Haruko's left side not only to press the walk signal button, but also now to be mindful of cars that might approach us from the left. I have always been mindful of which side I am on when walking with a woman. I never declare this aloud, but I am thinking it. In grade school a teacher had taught us that in medieval times people would often throw garbage and shit out of buildings onto the street, so it was courteous to walk on the street side of a woman so that the woman, walking nearest the building, would be less likely to be hit. Later, in the age of the automobile, the man would be a buffer between her and the street; between her and water splashing from tyres on a rainy day; between her and a car veering off the road.

So here I was walking on the side to which the cars were approaching. Oncoming traffic was not permitted to make a right-hand turn (from our perspective, a left turn, into us). There should have been no danger from the right, but only from the left. For that reason I was walking on Haruko's left. I could not have predicted, then, just as we were about to reach the other side of the road, that a driver would either ignore or not notice the rules of the intersection and turn directly into us from the oncoming lane. There was, on the other side of the intersection, something known as a "traffic bulge." It had a square-trimmed hedge-like shrub growing from it. Perhaps that is why he couldn't see us. It was, relatively, a low impact collision because the driver put on his brakes as soon as he noticed his mistake. Nevertheless, he collided with us — with Haruko first, because she had been walking on my right side. We fell like two dominos.

———————————

The accident was a silent happening — aside from the loud din of traffic, that is. It wasn't like in the movies at all. There was no symphonic burst, no reaction shots as the impact was about to happen. If there had been time to see the driver's face — well, that wouldn't have been possible, I'm sure; there would have been glare on the windshield. It was simply very quiet. The car came around the corner accelerating, but almost noiselessly. Haruko noticed, and in the split second prior to the collision, was able to turn slightly away. When the car hit her, she was at a slight angle to it, not perpendicular. This was a good thing, as a direct lateral impact might have damaged her right knee, if not both knees. From the very slight angle to which she was able to turn, her body had been better able to absorb the impact. Meanwhile, simultaneous to Haruko's reaction, the driver of the car had noticed us and slammed on the brakes. The car hit her with the force of a vigorous shove, and she fell into me. I fell, and put out my hands as I did so. Haruko rolled somehow — I didn't see.

We were on the ground, and I was getting up. The driver left his car where it had stopped, and approached us. I went to Haruko, who was still on the ground. The first thing the driver said was, "I am sorry. It's completely my fault. I'm not allowed to turn here." I think this is what he said. I think I remember it quite clearly, even if other aspects of this event remain unclear — the way Haruko tumbled, for example.

The events remain unclear — and more than that, they are grey. It was a smoky, soft-focus day to start, but the surprise of the accident seemed to turn down the chromatic saturation even further. I believe, for example, that the driver's car was in fact beige, but it seemed to me somehow grey. I remember it was a Ford Mondeo, which may have heightened the effect. Along with the Toyota Corolla, it is among the dullest cars ever designed. Such cars are not only appliance-like, but also surely a fit for Claus Luthe's "optical environmental pollution" criteria. A car like the Ford Mondeo always prompts me to wonder what kind of music one might possibly listen to when driving it. I can't imagine any music being heard in such a car. And this has always been how I assess the world. With people, too, I try to imagine their choice of music. With this driver, however — like his car — I couldn't imagine. He looked like someone exactly in the middle of his life. He was dressed neatly, yet in a nondescript way. Not casual, not too stylish. He seemed comfortable in his life — comfortable enough that he might occasionally disobey a traffic rule. He could cover it, it seems. The topic of insurance soon entered our discussion. He was articulate. He had a university education, I am sure, but I can't imagine what he might have studied.

Haruko told us she was feeling dizzy. She thought she might have hit her head, but she wasn't sure. She said her leg hurt — it might be bruised. The driver said she probably shouldn't move. He called the emergency number and gave our location. An ambulance was on its way. A witness came to us. "I saw clearly what happened," she said. She was grey, too. She had grey hair. She was like the "nice old lady" archetype of decades past. She was dressed in the clothes of an old lady some decades ago — not like an old lady of our time. I thought she might be insane. I also thought that the driver of the car might be insane, too. I was sure he never listened to music, and neither did the old lady. Or maybe I was the one who wasn't all right. And maybe Haruko, too. Finally I noticed my hands were stinging. There were red and white striations on the palms of my hands.

The ambulance arrived and the paramedics did a number of tests on Haruko. They told her she didn't have any obvious signs of a bone fracture, or of a "mild traumatic brain injury." She was able to walk, but they could take her to the hospital anyway, if she liked. She said she wouldn't need to visit the hospital. The paramedics advised her to put ice on her leg when she got home, and to call the emergency line immediately if she started vomiting. Then the "nice old lady," who had stayed with us the whole time, crumpled slowly to the ground. "I'm not feeling well," she said. "I think I might be having a heart attack."

19

I went back to the woods with the stairs down to the sea — the place I had first seen Haruko. (That is, "Haruko." I hadn't known at the time that she had once been "Agnieszka," whom I had met over a decade prior.) The wood was closed — the top of the stairway was closed. They had closed off the entranceway with a portable steel fence. Not just one piece, but many; they lengthened the fence to deter those who might go around. I went around anyway.

The fires were getting closer. Very close now. Not as intense as before — the news told me they were "ninety percent contained" — but closer. The city had closed off the woods in order to preserve them. Some of the outlying fires had been set intentionally, it seemed. But I had no intention of setting a fire. I had no desire to burn down the woods. I just wanted to enjoy them. Even if the fresh air was not so fresh.

I was wearing a gas mask — a Soviet-era GP-5 I found at a military surplus store. The Soviet Union no longer exists. The mask was surprisingly cheap. It was the real thing, I was told — although it had an aftermarket filter. I was told the original filters were unsafe. The GP-5 has round eyes. Nowadays, military gas masks don't have round eyes. So the mask made me feel as if I were reaching across to another era — not only of design, but of government. Now the Soviet Union no longer exists, except in the mind. The mask reminded me of the time traveller in H. G. Wells' *The Time Machine*; as strange as the flowers he brings from the future to show his dinner guests. Or as strange as one of the stone turtles at Karakorum, marking a city that now can only be imagined. The GP-5 gas mask should therefore have demanded a higher price. But my opinion of what is valuable, I think, is not an opinion commonly held. Additionally, the GP-5 mask was mass-produced continuously between 1962 and 1990, which may also be a factor.

The woods were still alive. I could hear the chirping of hummingbirds — Anna's hummingbirds, which are most common in this region. Not so much a chirping, but a clicking sound. I learned to recognize it in Ganbold's back yard. He had asked us to listen, and had shown me that sound for the first time. Since then I heard it frequently, but I had never heard it before. Now I was thinking of Ganbold as I descended the stairs. His backyard, on that day, had been so bright and green. This wood had been much the same, around that time. But I could see it was drying out. There were salal shrubs dotted throughout the wood, along the stairway. They had been pollinated — in part by the hummingbirds, I imagined — and had produced berries. But these berries were meagre and dry. Toward the bottom of the slope I noticed the tiny stream that normally flowed here had completely dried up, leaving just its imprint, barely damp veins to the edge of the foreshore.

What was I doing here, alone? Despite the smoke my children would enjoy it here, I thought. Aïsha would enjoy it here. We all could have brought our air filtration masks and enjoyed a day at the beach. I had been spending too much time away from them, and Aïsha was starting to get worried — and not just about my absences. Also about me. She had recently taken an interest in *feng shui*; there was more "chi energy" leaving me than I was taking in, she said. She rearranged the bedroom so that I could sleep with my head in the "calm, focussing" southwest, rather than the "stimulating" west, where it had been before. There were now plants in the bedroom, for "purification." A selenite pyramid on the windowsill, to dispel negative energy.

She had plans to change the flooring — to wood. (I hated the laminate flooring, too, but that's what the apartment came with, and we had been watching our money.) She told me she wanted to make our apartment "habitable" to me again. There was some unspeakable desperation in these measures. "Come back to us," she said. There was now something I was trying to force through my work with ND, she said. "And you know how things go when you force them — like with your band." I wasn't so sure about that, exactly, but I could feel she was right on some level. Yes, maybe things had gone sideways. They had. But I couldn't just get out of it now. Not right away. It wouldn't be long now, though. Simply, I needed to finish what I'd started. So I went to the trail alone. To the ocean. To consider the next steps...

When I arrived at the bottom of the stairs, the foreshore was almost completely exposed. I had chosen this day, and this time, for an unusually low tide — just 0.55 meters. The beach was now a wide band of hard-packed damp sand. It was dotted with small indentations where burrowing molluscs had retracted their siphons. They seemed to thrive, despite the smoke. It was hazy, and I wondered if these bivalves (called bivalves because their shells have two halves connected with a hinge) even noticed. I am sure the air quality must have some effect even on bivalve molluscs (razor clams, in this case, I thought) buried in the sand. I thought about the awareness of such animals in their sandy encasements. And I thought about my own awareness — things of which I was aware or not aware or might affect me or not.

There was a smooth boulder in the sand, about as tall as a chairback, at a comfortable incline. I reclined against it, regarding it with my sense of touch: its smooth, cool surface against my back. I observed, too, the feeling of hard damp sand on my buttocks, on the backs of my legs. I was now completely unclothed aside from the gas mask, and I sat there gazing at the sea through its round eyeholes, and through the haze, which I imagined as mist. Occasionally there were sparkles on the waves. Soft focus sparkles on wavelets seen through the "mist."

Distantly I could see the outline of a boat moving toward the inlet — moving toward the port. It was a calm ocean, and the boat was sailing at a calm pace. I could tell from its outline that it was one of those large marine vessels known as a *car carrier*.

I knew there would be a lot of cars on that big ship.

Copyeditor's Interjection

The third missive in the original publisher's file for Naked Defiance *is from an apparent copyeditor, who writes: "It was hard for me to perform even the most banal editing tasks on a manuscript that I frankly couldn't tolerate — nevertheless, I thank you for paying me a rate above the industry standard. And if you don't mind me telling you — for your sake, although I couldn't care less about the author — I would strongly advise adding one of those 'work of fiction' legal disclaimers." She adds that to help her "recover from the [copyediting] experience," she wrote a supplementary passage "much in the spirit of those supplied by the author" and attached it "just to let you know how strongly I feel." She invites the publisher to use it but acknowledges he "probably won't." Here I have taken the liberty to include the passage, which follows. –PS*

Hello. I'm the new author — another author. An editor, in fact. I've been tasked with editing this book. I'm taking over for the old editor — Florian — who just got sacked. To be honest, he had never exactly been hired in the first place, but he was certainly fired. Or at least I'm taking over at this point, and you can guess who I am. I've been gradually introducing my hand, in case you hadn't noticed. Undoubtedly, this is still Florian's book — the basic outline, the narrator's voice. But now I have a hand on the steering wheel, and I'm going to make sure this story goes where it needs to go. Can you see why? I'm sure you can see why. I'm sure you can see why this story needs a defter hand. Florian made an attempt to steer it right, but I can tell you he certainly failed at that, so now I'm taking over — a bit.

Until now this book has lacked coherence. A story needs coherence. Even more than that, it needs adherence. It needs answers. Florian attempted to provide some answers, but raised a singular doubt: that he in fact knows what an answer is. And this story needs answers, quickly. And I have them. I have the answers. Better yet, I have the problems to the answers. Because once you have an answer (which I do) you must identify the problem.

One particular objection I've had to this story so far was the way it — the way he, the author — makes light of the Siege of Kiev. Can you imagine what it would have been like to have been one of the victims? I mean, locked inside the Church of Tithes, waiting for the inevitable, completely surrounded, knowing the invaders would show no mercy to anyone… Can you imagine what it would be like to die that way? It would be like being on the Titanic — but worse. Have you seen that movie, *Titanic*? It's about the same thing — people waiting to die. It stars Leonardo DiCaprio. I felt sad in that movie when he died. Mostly. He's some kind of environmentalist. That's a good thing, maybe. Environmentalism is one answer. But there are other things, other answers, that need to be given first.

One thing that makes life bearable is not knowing when you will die. If you knew when you would die, you would be immortal. Someone says that in a film by Tarkovsky. I think it was *Solaris*, but I could be wrong. I didn't know much about Tarkovsky until I started reading this book. The author — Florian, or whoever — is a big fan of Tarkovsky. Tarkovsky was Russian, and the Russians caused the Holodomor. And Tarkovsky also had to have one scene in almost every film — perhaps not *The Mirror* — with a woman wearing something rather sheer, or thin, and obviously not wearing a bra underneath — but not because bras weren't available in the Soviet Union, I can tell you … And she's having a kind of "sexualized fit." That's Geoff

Dyer's term for it, and he wrote a book in which lots of body parts are called by name... and I don't like that. Not one bit. Do you see where all this is coming from? Where it's going?

If you can just stand by when there's a problem, and just doubt and doubt and doubt, then clearly you're part of the problem. George W. Bush said that. He said, "Either you are with us, or you are with the terrorists." Now, I'm not a big fan of George W. Bush. Just in the same way I said I'm not a big fan of Stalin — that's true. And it's also certainly true who did the terrorizing in this book. Ganbold did it, and I have no use for idiots who, despite all the evidence, want to keep searching for more evidence. How much more do you need? When we know something, we know something. There was enough to go on, there should have been no holding back. The crime should have been balanced right away. I think Florian was holding back just because he wanted to get to his word count, or whatever. Delaying for such a crass purpose only adds further insult to the injury. Whenever something happens, the balance has to come — the sooner the better. And whether the crime was yesterday, ten years ago, or 800 years ago, it still needs to be balanced. There has to be some balance in this world. And let me tell you, there's going to be some balancing. Now. Soon. In this book.

Until now I've made only a few minor additions to this story — to tilt the wheel, ever so slightly, in the right direction. It's been quite subtle, I think. The only very obvious thing I've changed was the section titles. They were numbered at first, then I renamed them "Spring," "Summer," and "Fall." And here's where I really put my mark on the story. (Not too much, of course, but just enough. As much as the publisher will allow.) In this final section you're going to see — you're going to read — why "Fall" is certainly apt. To make sure everyone gets what they deserve — to make sure Florian gets what he deserves. For just standing by and not answering the problem.

But enough of that. Enough justification. Enough rationale. Let's not delay. Let's get straight back to the story. Back to "Florian." Now we read, in his own words, how he learns what he gets.

FALL

20

"Good, good. Your pupils are contracting just as we'd expect."

Haruko aimed the flashlight away from my face and turned it off. The white light dissipated quickly, and her face faded into view. She was quite close to me, looking into my eyes. She wasn't looking at me as a whole, but looking into each eye in turn, in isolation. I was sitting on the edge of a kitchen table. Its melamine resin surface felt cool on my bare thighs. I was wearing nothing but a hospital dressing gown, tied at the back. It was a lighter shade of the same colour as the table top: cyan. (I imagined that such a colour might have been marketed as "aqua.")

"Now we're going to test some of your other reflexes."

"How many more?" I asked.

"Just a few more. I know we've done a lot of tests, but we're almost at the end."

She hit just below my right knee with a tiny rubber hammer, and my leg kicked involuntarily. She did the same to the other side, and there was the same reaction.

"Excellent. Everything's working properly so far. Now raise your right arm and put it straight out in front of you, palm down. I'm going to press down, and I want you to resist me."

She pressed down and my arm bounced slightly, but remained level.

"Good. Good strong resistance. Now try this."

She removed an eyedropper from a small brown glass vial.

"What is it?"

"It's just honey and salt. I'm going to put it under your tongue."
I opened my mouth so she could do so.

"Now we're going to try the same thing. Put out your arm."
I put out my arm, she pressed down on it, and it was noticeably weaker.

"Interesting, right?" she said.

"Yes. How does that work?"

"It's hard to explain, but your body responded as it should. So far so good."

"But why are we doing this? What are you testing?"

"I'm testing all of your reflexes — or as many as I can without being too invasive. After someone has experienced a disquieting event, like you have — like we have — we need to test all the reflexes to best determine a line of treatment."

"Treatment? How do you know all this?"

"I'm a neuro reflex therapist — an NRT. I thought you knew."

"No. I don't think you told me."

"But I'm sure I told you. Yes, I'm an NRT."

"How does one become an NRT?"

"Well, first you have to take a nursing degree —"

"You're a nurse?"

"Yes! Really, I thought you knew all that. Yes. I am a nurse. I was a nurse. I was working as a nurse, and then I studied an extra year to become an NRT. I got tired of all the shit and piss and blood and face masks and doctors and hospitals and clinics and disposable sterile gloves — although I did take a few of the patient gowns with me. Anyway, I was sick of it all, and I just wanted to help people for a change. And work on my own. But mostly I wanted to help people. And now I want to help you. And I want to help me. Because we've both experienced something very... very shocking, terrifying. We both need help right now. And now I'm testing you — to determine the best treatment, to help you recover. And there are just a few more tests to go. Maybe two tests. Or three. Next, I want you to lie down, face up on this bed."

In the same room was a Murphy bed, which Haruko pulled down from the wall. It had crisp white sheets tucked tightly into its sides. I lay down on it, face up as instructed. The mattress was quite firm.

"You've tested quite well, so far," she said. "That means you're quite resilient."

She reached over and started rolling up the hem of my hospital gown until it was just below my navel.

"What are you doing?" I asked.

"We have to test a few more things: tightening reflex, rate of tumescence —"

"What? I think that's all working fine," I said.

"Maybe. But we still need to test."

"That seems a bit personal," I said.

"If you like I can use disposable sterile gloves."

"It's not a matter of not trusting your hygiene," I said. "It's just that it's a bit... personal. I mean, if my wife saw me here... with a woman about to test me this way..."

"Does this feel intimate to you, Florian?"

"Well, in a way, yes. It feels like —"

"You don't want to feel like you are cheating on your wife. I know. You told me. And to you, being like this is very close to your person, with —"

"Exactly."

"You're overthinking this, Florian. Your wife will understand. This is a medical test. I'm a married woman, too. I would understand. If my husband were having a test like this. There's nothing intimate or personal about it. It's purely a medical test. Your wife wants what's best for you, doesn't she? I'm sure she wants you to get the best treatment possible. And I can't prescribe a treatment until I've done all the tests. So, I'm going to do all the tests, and you have nothing to worry about."

"Are you sure?"

"As a medical professional I am obliged to do a thorough examination. If something is wrong, you want to know. I know you do."

"So how is it going to work?"

"Would you say you are more visually stimulated, or do you rely more on your tactile sense?"

"Visually, maybe."

"Have you seen Dalí's Gala portrait?"

"I'm not sure. Although I probably should know. I have a degree in art history."

"Well, I can pose like Gala and maybe you'll remember... and that way perhaps I can gauge your response. She posed like this."

"Oh. That's not one of his portraits I know."

"And I've forgotten to bring some of my equipment — the tools I do for these tests. But I've been needing to test some of my own reflexes, too. So if you don't mind I'm going to use the 'direct experience' method."

"Direct experience?"

"I'm sure you wouldn't want me using the tools, anyway. Sometimes it's the human body itself that takes the most accurate readings. I mean, would you go to a physiotherapist who moves your limbs around with a pair of iron tongs?"

21

I was awakened by a loud, hollow sound. It was as if a team of Shire horses had been momentarily lowered to the roof from a dirigible — as if they had been lowered using a pulley system and then raised just a moment later. Or it might have been a phonograph record — a recording of Shire horses running on a hollow surface in a narrow, wooded canyon. It was as if the needle of the record player had been lowered, then raised a moment later. It was not the sound of pounding hooves approaching from a distance, then fading out into another distance. It was sudden, and momentary, and it sounded as if it were on the roof.

It was early dawn. I was in the Murphy bed, and Haruko was in the adjacent galley kitchen. She was standing at the stove, facing my direction. She was peering down at a moka pot. Its lid was opened; she seemed to be inspecting its collecting chamber. The stove element was glowing orange. Haruko was dressed as if to go out — she had clearly been up for a while. I noticed I was wearing a pair of cotton pajamas. My wife had given them to me as a birthday present. Normally I didn't wear pajamas in bed.

"You're up," said Haruko.

"Good morning," I replied.

"You must have slept well."

"I'm not sure. I had a very strange dream last night."

"Oh?"

"You and I… We were testing our bodies, and —"

"Yes, I know. I think I had the same dream." Haruko's gaze remain focussed on the moka pot, and presently a smile came over her face — like a smile of satisfaction or contentment. She continued, "Now it's happening."

"What?"

"My morning ritual. I know it might seem funny, but every morning I have to do this. I like to be there just as the coffee starts flowing out of the spigot. Just at that very moment. These are the best kind of coffee pots. And I don't mean just this kind. I mean this particular model. The Bialetti Venus. I switched to stainless steel some years ago when there was that scare about aluminum and dementia — although I think that's been debunked. Anyway, it's very simple. Very durable. I've had other pots that fell apart, but not this one. I know you appreciate design."

"There are a lot of famous things from Italy."

"You know, I can't believe you slept through all that commotion last night."

"What commotion?"

"The crackling fire. The sirens. They were spraying the walls of our building so it wouldn't catch. That man screaming 'Help me, help me! Please won't you help me?' until someone brought a ladder. Sorrowful wailing. And then someone was pounding on the door, asking if anyone was here. Telling us that if we were here, to get out. I pretended not to notice."

"What happened?"

"The restaurant. Where we ate last night. It burned down. Completely. You should look."

I got up from the Murphy bed and went to the window. The glass was warped, and also foggy, so I opened it to get a clear view. It was one of those old wood-framed windows with a vertically sliding bottom pane, balanced with internal counterweights on a fixed pulley. It still worked smoothly. Outside, two doors down across the gravel intersection, I could see the charred remains of the restaurant. The building had collapsed in on itself, and was now a pile of smouldering rubble. A solitary firefighter was still there, hosing it down.

"This town is disappearing. There seems to be one less building every time I visit," I said.

"They won't rebuild it," Haruko replied. "I heard someone say they had no insurance."

"If they ever build something there again, it's sure to be ugly."

I remained at the window, surveying the ruins, and the small town. Its backdrop was a rocky hill of sparse pine — above that, swiftly moving clouds against the dawn sky. It was a bright, full moon, still visible in the morning. At first I thought it might be a kind of street light, or a kind of weather balloon, illuminated internally. That is because, as the clouds floated past, this "moon" seemed to be in front of them. I thought, surely it must be an optical illusion. But the longer I looked, the more apparent it became this was in fact no mirage: the moon was in front of the clouds.

We had arrived the previous day. The forest fires had subsided and travel again was permitted into the interior. In memory of Ganbold, we were to perform one last action, and we had chosen this location — this dissipating town in the mountains, some five hours away by car. We had rented a room in a two-storey hotel. We were the hotel's only occupants. Some fifty years previously, the same building had been the town's firehall. (I wondered if, had the town retained this location, the firefighters might have arrived to the restaurant in time to save it.)

Like the hotel, the restaurant was in a building that had been repurposed, or so it seemed. In its symmetrical façade were two inset entrances — as if it had once been two smaller shops, side by side. Inside was a row of pillars that must once have framed a wall bisecting the tall-ceilinged main floor. The waitress had us seated at a table for two that had been pushed against the double doors of one of the entrances. On the outside of these doors was a sign that read, "Please use other door." We asked to move to another table. There were other options. When we arrived we had been the only customers aside from a woman with three elementary-aged children, none of whom seemed related, seated near the back of the restaurant near the kitchen's serving window, playing a board game. The restaurant had a shelf of board games for customers.

Our action had been to converse, publicly, in idioglossia. When the waitress took our order, I "interpreted" for Haruko. This had been Haruko's idea. Compared to all the actions I had heard about, or taken part in, this was certainly not one I could claim to love — but I didn't have any better ideas. Rather than surprising our audience — in this case, our waitress — with something "just a little bit marvelous" (this was Ganbold's phrase) it felt like we were mocking them. I wondered why I felt that way, and how I might articulate the difference between this action and another — say, walking through a forest while wearing a strange outfit.

Another customer had entered the restaurant. He looked like a truck driver, but I can't verify this was in fact the case, because we saw no truck. Immediately he walked to the jukebox — the restaurant had a large, battered jukebox — and flipped through the selections. He must have been a regular. As he stood at the jukebox, the waitress handed him a menu directly. "Why don't you get some new music on this thing?" he asked. "Or at least something everyone knows. April Wine. The Eagles. At least that song, 'Take It Easy.' I like that song a lot. Anything but this shit." The waitress simply smiled, then continued to our table, where she cleared our dishes.

The entire time we were in the restaurant, the jukebox had been playing a series of pop songs that all seemed to come from a certain time, in a certain style, by performers whose stars had shone, then faded: Sandra, Laura Branigan, Kano, Endgames, Bandolero, Desireless, Chemise, Jeanne Mas. The jukebox had been exported from Austria to the Ukraine, we were told, not long after the fall of the iron curtain. Then somehow it ended up here. I thought to myself: if only, in my music career, I had been a few years earlier...

22

On the drive back (I had rented a car), Haruko told me the story of the Aarhus Air Raid, and her great uncle. He was the youngest of three children, she said, the little brother of her paternal grandfather. He was an apprentice carpenter and an aspiring architect, and had visited the University of Aarhus on October 31, 1944, in an attempt to meet Christian Frederik Møller (no relation), the university's main architect, who had that morning been surveying work on the university's main building.

At the time, Aarhus University was serving as headquarters for the Gestapo, which had recently weakened the Danish resistance after its operations were exposed by a British paratrooper confessing under torture as well as by Grethe Bartram, Gestapo informant and sister to resistance operative Christian, who had divulged to her some of his work. Out of desperation, Vagn Bennike, chief of resistance in Jutland, telegrammed London requesting the aerial bombardment of specified locations at the university campus where the Gestapo — and three resistance prisoners — were being housed. Within a week, the request was obliged.

At 11:41 a.m. on the appointed day, the first bombs, supplied by two dozen Mosquito Mark VI fighter bombers, exploded at the campus. The bombing was supposed to be very accurate to mitigate civilian deaths. A reconnaissance mission had been made five days previously, and that was followed by practice runs taken at a full-scale target outline drawn with chalk. Because the attack was to be made at such a low elevation, there was a chance the aircraft could be damaged by the explosions, and for this reason the bombs were set with an eleven-second delay. Unfortunately for Haruko's great uncle, this was long enough for a stray bomb to enter the main building and slide along the floor to where he happened to be.

"Life is a path we follow in a single direction," said Haruko, "and my great uncle's path was very short. He had aspirations. He had a girlfriend. Perhaps they were thinking of marriage. The war was almost over, he thought, and then he would get on with his life. And then, for him, there was nothing. A short life is generally unremarkable. And now, to be sure, no one even knows his name, apart from my family. He's just one of 'ten civilian casualties' in a Wikipedia entry."

"It's not fair," I said. "It's very sad."

"It's not fair, and it's sad. But who takes responsibility? I was at a museum recently, and I learned there was a lumber mill near where I was born, that produced Douglas fir components for the wings of Mosquito bombers. The write-up in the museum referred to the 'war effort,' and was quite favourable. The aircraft's main designer, I think, was a man named Geoffrey de Havilland."

"The Mosquito was very well designed. Have you seen it?"

"There was the designing, the financing, the testing, the resources supplied. And then there were the pilots."

"My own great uncle was a pilot. And I am sorry to say he was the pilot of a Mosquito bomber that took part in the Aarhus Air Raid."

"I know it. I did my research."

"Really?"

"Did you ever meet your great uncle?"

"No."

"I wonder what someone like that was thinking. Someone who takes part in a bombing raid. I wonder what your great uncle was thinking as he prepared for the raid. Perhaps he thought: if there's a war someone has to die. If there's a gun it has to shoot."

"From what I understand, he had always wanted to be a pilot."

"And after the war?"

"According to my father, he became a real estate agent, and he owned a house by the ocean, with a swimming pool at the edge of the water, supplied by the tide."

"That's nice. How did your family feel about him?"

"I think he was admired, generally. I think they looked at him as a war hero. Apparently he was quite an amiable guy."

"I don't blame him, you know."

"For having a swimming pool?"

"No — for killing my own great uncle."

"Well, we don't know for sure that the bombs he dropped —"

"You see, war is a terrible, terrible thing. It makes people betray one another. Innocent people are hurt, or killed. That's just the way it is. It's mindless — but I don't mean that in the pejorative sense. Not necessarily. Someone needs a job, so they work at a factory making bombs. Someone wants to be a pilot, and they end up flying an aircraft that drops the bombs. And what does it matter? They defeated Hitler, didn't they? Whether they had any thoughts about Hitler one way or another."

"I understand he was a good employer. He took good care of his secretary, Traudl Junge. She said so. She said he liked to work in a cold room, but he gave her a heater —"

"They say that in war the end justifies the means."

"Yes, that's what they say."

"Tell me, Florian: have you ever felt that in some way, at some level, you're part of a war; that there's a war going on, and you're one actor?"

"I'm not sure, but I suppose —"

"Have you ever noticed that wherever you go — wherever we go — there's something falling apart? That things seem to be burning?"

23

When Haruko and I parted ways, I felt strangely afraid. She told me that leaving Defiance marked the end of a certain time in her life that she associated with the name "Haruko" — that she could no longer carry on with that name. "Its associations are a burden for me now," she said. "I might go back to 'Agnieszka' — or maybe I shouldn't. No. I should really find a new name. For a new life. Anastasia... Renée... Or should it be Danuta or Jadwiga? I have to give it some thought." She told me never again to call her by the name "Haruko." Soon she would go by a new name, but the transformation would take time. That I should wait until she was ready. She would contact me when she was ready.

When I arrived home it was late in the day, around the time I normally had dinner with my family. They weren't home, so I went to the balcony. There were some new potted plants, arranged in a particular way. Feng shui, I though. On the balcony I sat on a small bench, and looked down onto the street. Our building was tall for the area, our apartment was on a high floor, and I had a clear vantage of all before me. It was early autumn, and still quite light at that time of day. The sun was going down somewhere slightly behind me, to my right. The street was well illuminated, and what stood out to me most was a sign — a large, bright white sign. It seemed new, and must have been put up while I was away. It was perhaps two by three meters, probably corrugated plastic, stapled to a makeshift wood frame. I couldn't read the fine print from my distance, but the title was: DEVELOPMENT PROPOSAL. It seemed to refer to the building directly in front of me. It was a fine building. It must have been a very fine building one hundred years ago, when it was built. The year was set in stained glass above the door in the arched entranceway. It had bay windows. Three storeys. Iron fire escapes, some of which were rusting. There was a blue tarp covering a hole in the roof. The building had been left to decay — intentionally, I thought.

From the same building, a man stepped out onto the second-floor fire escape. He pulled a bicycle through the door, then lowered it down from the side of the fire escape to another man waiting below. Strange, I thought. Why not just send it out the front door? I had a direct view, too, of other buildings across the way, into the bedrooms and living rooms of numerous apartments. In one, a man was dancing with a standalone wooden coat rack, twirling around it. He held it, gave it a dip, then kissed it. Elsewhere, on the pavement below, a woman was smoking a cigarette, pacing. A car drove up beside her. She exchanged some words with the driver and pointed down the street. The car drove away.

The balcony door was open, and I could hear into our apartment. I could hear the squeals of children fading into audible range from the hallway. I could hear Travel, and Trudi. They sounded excited, happy. I heard the voice of Aïsha, too. I heard the lock turn, and the door open. Aïsha reminded the children to put their shoes away, to wash their hands. I heard these sounds, and they mingled with my recollection of the previous two days, with my view across the street... Just as in a piece of music in which a particular timbre, preamble, and combination of notes can induce tears, all these mingled observations were about to do the same.

I could tell you more. I could draw this out to induce in you the same physiological sensations. Perhaps you can already imagine how I felt. Or maybe you can't, or you're not feeling it. No. I imagine you can't feel it. You probably feel nothing at all for me. I wonder if you can — or even if you should — empathize with me. Needless to say, I empathize with me. And I think you at least know — even if it induces no compassionate response — what happened to me. It was precisely at that moment I knew what happened to me, too. I couldn't fill my lungs smoothly or completely, and thought I might start weeping. I didn't want my family to see me weeping. I stood up. I tried to control my breathing...

EPILOGUE

Ganbold Mirzoyan (1951- ▮)
Ganbold Mirzoyan died in police custody. At the time of death, Mirzoyan was in his jail cell, being questioned by an unnamed police constable. They were the only occupants of the jail cell at the time, and there were no witnesses. An autopsy confirmed that Mirzoyan was killed by a single bullet, which had entered the back of his head. His death was the subject of an internal police investigation, which determined the constable had shot Mirzoyan "in self-defence." An officer present at the investigation reported the constable's testimony to have been "a studied exercise in the use of one- and two-syllable words, exclusively — almost like some kind of performance art." The one exception was his answer to the question posed by an assistant deputy commissioner, who led the investigation. That is, why had he felt it necessary to use lethal force? To this, the constable answered: "Because, sir, he expatiated too much." The assistant deputy commissioner remarked that it must have been a "very heavy decision" to use lethal force, and that it was "understandable to act that way, when someone expatiates too much."

Solomiya Gura (1965-20–)
Following the death of Ganbold Mirzoyan, Solomiya Gura became the eminent figure in Naked Defiance, which she disbanded approximately one year later. From that point forward, apart from a brief copyediting stint at a local book publisher,

she focussed almost entirely on her communications work for the local branch of an NGO. As the result of her high-profile advocacy, she was eventually hired by a state government, and rose quickly to the rank of Deputy Minister for Equality and Fairness. In this capacity she worked tirelessly — on average, sixteen hours per day. She developed a number of health problems, but worked through them, such was her devotion to public service. During her career she played no small role in an apparent corruption scandal, after which the minister resigned, a number of low-ranking officials were dismissed, and another was driven to suicide. She then survived a court case instigated by the family of the suicide victim (against whom no charges had been laid, but who was "evidently culpable" in Gura's words) and was publicly lauded by the state governor for her "steadfast allegiance to propriety and justice." During her long and decorated career, which lasted well past the customary age of retirement, she took only one vacation: a guided tour of Crimea. There, a tour guide noted her "expert interest" in some of the 14th century ruins around Staryi Krym, where she held her hands up in prayer and recited: "Let these vermin be abandoned to themselves until all have perished — until we, the chosen people, rightfully take our place in the land." The tour guide's emotions were evidently stirred by the gesture, and he reported "a feeling of enchantment, of being transported into past times." In a single instant, he said, "centuries of mist were lifted, and dry historical record became living reality." From this unique event he was "readily able to draw inferences" that would later be put to use in a successful political career.

Florian Moore (1963-█████)

Florian Moore retrained as an automotive mechanic and founded a successful business that specialized in reconditioning rare European cars of the 1960s and 1970s. As his personal vehicle, he reconditioned a 1977 Isuzu 117, which according to his diary, he felt had "sufficient European content," having been designed by Giorgetto Giugiaro. (Moreover, he noted, the 117's companion model was called the Florian.) In his garage he stocked a disproportionately vast number of items particular to the Citroën SM and the NSU Ro 80. These pieces included a Ford Essex V4 engine, which had been used as a replacement for the Ro 80's notoriously unreliable rotary motor. His diary also revealed his hope that, as one of the few vintage European car specialists in the area, he might inevitably cross paths with Altantsetseg and Sergiy Vynnychenko, with whom he wished "to make amends."

While establishing his career as an automotive mechanic, Florian Moore became a voracious reader of Hitler biographies, and involved himself in a group called Aryan Warriors for Christ (AWC), which had been founded by Joseph P. White, previously known for his "Christian rock" remakes of albums by Kajagoogoo and Scritti Politti. ("Crucified," White's remake of the latter group's "Hypnotize," had reached the top twenty on Billboard's "Hot Christian Songs" chart.) Florian's membership in AWC caused unresolvable tension with his wife, Aïsha, who, although agnostic, was of maternal Ethiopian Jewish and paternal Bosnian Muslim ancestry. Aïsha and Florian ultimately separated, their children living with the former. According to Aïsha Moore, her husband had attempted to save the marriage, insisting that his conversion to Nazism was "nothing personal," that he still loved her and their children, that he was a "Nazi gradualist" who saw his children eventually "mating" with pure Aryans to "gradually purify the nation" over a number of generations. A diary entry sheds light on how his erstwhile presumed pseudo-Marxism was reconciled with his newfound interest in racial purity: "I am convinced," he wrote, "that only the nation, united by race and religion, has the strength to overcome transnational spectacular capitalism."

After the separation, Moore rarely visited his family, and the last time they met him he was, according to Aïsha, "literally a different person. Although he looked like Florian, his body was merely a shell. It was as if his body had been reanimated by someone else entirely — or something even stranger." She reported that he seemed "like a completely different kind of animal, even — a non-human, in the same way a hummingbird hawk-moth is a non-hummingbird, even though they look the same from a distance." She reported feeling "terrified" by this uncanny parallelism. It was as if, she said, his face contained all the elements of a human face, but for completely different purposes. His eyes, for example, "seemed like those fake eyes on the backs of some caterpillars." Moreover, his language seemed distant. "He spoke our language," said Aïsha, "but I began to feel that only the sounds were the same, that maybe he was speaking a completely different language in which the words and grammar sounded the same, but pointed to something exactly different." Her fear, during this last meeting, was so intense that she "froze on the spot," disengaged from the conversation, and waited until Florian had exhausted his words, afraid of what he might do if she asked him to leave. When he finally did leave, Aïsha "vowed never to speak to him again."

Roughly two years after this last meeting, Florian Moore was found dead in his garage at the time of a large-scale coronavirus outbreak. An autopsy was performed, but the ultimate cause of death was unclear. At the time of death he had been infected by the coronavirus, but he also appeared to have been afflicted with a rare and slow-to-progress brain-wasting disease — and had suffered a degree of carbon monoxide poisoning, as well. The cause of death may have been suicide, as it appears the engine of his Isuzu 117 had been left running while the car was inside the garage, with the garage door closed. (The keys were in the ignition turned to the "ON" position, the gasoline tank was empty.) However, as the coroner was obliged to indicate only one cause, Florian Moore's death certificate indicates "Coronavirus."

Haruko Agnieszka Rusakova, née Møller (1968-20??)

Not long after Haruko Rusakova abandoned Naked Defiance, her husband, Dmitry Rusakov, retired from his job as an aircraft mechanic. To celebrate his retirement, Rusakov bought two round-the-world air tickets so that he and Haruko could embark on a "dream vacation." The point of this vacation was to visit a number of crash sites where high-ranking politicians had lost their lives, as well as the museums which housed extant examples of related aircraft. Two incidents in particular had fascinated Dmitry Rusakov: the 1961 presumed assassination of United Nations Secretary-General Dag Hammarkjöld, and the political flight of Lin Biao, Vice Chairman of the Communist Party of China, almost exactly ten years later in 1971.

At the National Museum of the United States Air Force, in Dayton, Ohio, the Rusakovs viewed a Douglas DC-6 airliner, similar to the one that had carried Dag Hammarskjöld when it crashed near Ndola, in what is now Zambia. Also in the United States, they visited a private collector to view a Fouga CM.170 Magister. This is the aircraft flown by Belgian-British mercenary Jan van Risseghem when it is believed he shot down the DC-6. Despite a decoy airliner being sent on a different route (it was known an assassination attempt might be made against Hammarskjöld), van Risseghem was able to find the correct aircraft. He had been working for the short-lived State of Katanga, which had broken away from the Congo, and was apparently bankrolled by a Belgian mining company. Hammarskjöld had been on his way to negotiate a ceasefire in the Congo. The Rusakovs also visited the crash site in Zambia, then spent some time in Europe, visiting relatives.

From Europe, they took a flight to Beijing. While there, they visited the Military Museum of the Chinese People's Revolution in order to view a Hawker Siddeley Trident airliner similar to the aircraft in which Lin Biao lost his life. Either in the aftermath of an aborted coup d'état against then Chairman Mao Zedong, or because he knew he was about to be purged, Lin left the country in a Trident, along with members of his family. It is assumed his intention was to defect to the Soviet Union. Strangely, at its crash site in Mongolia, the aircraft was discovered facing the opposite direction.

After an overnight train to Ulaanbaatar, the Rusakovs rented a UAZ-452 off-road van, which they intended to drive to Öndörkhaan, crash site of Lin's Trident airliner. The UAZ was found abandoned north of Öndörkhaan, near the presumed burial place of Chingis Khan. At the time of their visit, Brethren of the Khan, a self-declared "men's therapy group," was holding a rally in the area. With a mandate to "defend the grave of our nation's founder," the Brethren are known to be overtly sexist, xenophobic, antisemitic, anti-gay, against labour unions, pro-capitalist, and very right wing. They are also known to hate Chinese, Japanese, and Russians (with the exception of Baron Roman Fyodorovich von Ungern-Sternberg), and are fond of Harley-Davidson motorcycles, the "Stainless Banner" of the Confederate States of America, and swastikas. Although suspected in the disappearance of Haruko and Dmitry Rusakov, the Brethren of the Khan have not claimed responsibility, nor have any witnesses come forward.

BLAP!